"My apologies for interrupting your afternoon delight."

"Nothing happened," Madeline said for the umpteenth time to anyone who would listen.

Suddenly, Russell's smooth baritone floated into the room. "I thought something happened."

Everyone whipped around and made a collective gasp at the polished *GQ* ghost of Russell Stone. He stepped through the archway, eyes locked on Madeline.

Everyone, except his wife, crowded around him in approval of his transformation.

Everything about him was exactly the same…except for the eyes. Still a rich sable, but the soul within was damaged. And for the first time Madeline wondered what the past six years had been like for him. To be lost. To not know who you are.

Russell smiled.

Madeline smiled back.

Madeline assessed his low-cropped hair with its smooth, even manicured lines, his creamy, milk-chocolate skin, his broad but lean physique, and finally came to terms with the truth—Russell Stone had returned. Brick by brick, the walls of her defenses crumbled to the ground, and she'd never been more scared in her life.

D0424610

Books by Adrianne Byrd

Kimani Romance

She's My Baby
When Valentines Collide
To Love a Stranger

Kimani Arabesque

When You Were Mine
Takin' Chances for the Holidays
"Finding the Right Key"
A Season of Miracles
"Wishing on a Star"

ADRIANNE BYRD

has always preferred to live within the realm of her imagination, where all the men are gorgeous and the women are worth whatever trouble they manage to get into.

TO LOVE A STRANGER

ADRIANNE BYRD

KIMANI
ROMANCE

If you purchased this book without a cover you should be aware
that this book is stolen property. It was reported as "unsold and
destroyed" to the publisher, and neither the author nor the
publisher has received any payment for this "stripped book."

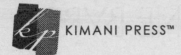

KIMANI PRESS™

ISBN-13: 978-0-373-86044-9
ISBN-10: 0-373-86044-7

TO LOVE A STRANGER

Copyright © 2007 by Adrianne Byrd

All rights reserved. The reproduction, transmission or utilization
of this work in whole or in part in any form by any electronic, mechanical
or other means, now known or hereafter invented, including xerography,
photocopying and recording, or in any information storage or retrieval
system, is forbidden without written permission. For permission please
contact Kimani Press, Editorial Office, 233 Broadway, New York, NY
10279 U.S.A.

This is a work of fiction. Names, characters, places and incidents are
either the product of the author's imagination or are used fictitiously,
and any resemblance to actual persons, living or dead, business establishments,
events or locales is entirely coincidental.

® and TM are trademarks. Trademarks indicated with ® are registered in
the United States Patent and Trademark Office, the Canadian Trade Marks
Office and/or other countries.

www.kimanipress.com

Printed in U.S.A.

Dear Reader,

I hope you enjoy *To Love a Stranger*. I actually had this story idea for a few years. One of my favorite films is *Sommersby* and one of my favorite songs is "Stranger in My House" by Tamia. However, the story resurfaced in my mind when I read an article about U.K. news on the Internet. The heading asked: *Do you know this man?*

The story was about a mysterious man who'd refused to speak since he'd been found wandering on a windswept road on the Isle of Sheppey. Eventually they gave the man pencil and paper and he sketched a piano. Excited, the hospital staff directed him to a room where there was a piano, and he began playing. He was dubbed the piano man, but doctors and nurses had nothing else to help identify their mysterious patient.

So this had me thinking....

Prologue

November 23, 2001

"The baby is still breached," Dr. Roberts announced to his small crew in the obstetrical ward. "Let's get her prepped for an emergency C-section."

An elevated Madeline Stone lay huffing and puffing on the delivery table wondering where in the hell was the epidural.

"Okay, Mrs. Stone. I need you to *stop* pushing for me."

She would if she could, but in truth she had no

control over what was going on in her lower extremities. It was all she could do to ride out the waves of muscle spasms, sharp stabs of back pain and the streams of sweat burning her eyes.

Madeline's best friend and second cousin, Lysandra Hobbs, burst into the delivery room in a pair of blue scrubs. "I'm here. I'm here. I made it!"

Madeline responded with a high-pitched scream followed by a low rabid growl. No doubt about it; the baby she carried was determined to split her in half.

What in the hell was she doing here? And why wasn't her ass of a husband there so she could rip his penis off for knocking her up for the second time.

Then again, why was she surprised? He wasn't around when she delivered their son two years ago, either. Madeline made a vow right then and there to shoot her husband if he ever came near her bed again. Better yet, maybe it was time to file for divorce. To hell with the prenuptial agreement.

"Breathe," Lysandra coached, rushing to her side and taking Madeline's hand. However, with one mighty squeeze, Madeline crushed Lysandra's frail fingers and forced her cousin to her knees.

"I'm going to kill him," Madeline snarled

through yet another contraction. "I know he's with that hussy."

All heads swiveled in Madeline's direction, but censuring her words was something else she couldn't manage at the moment.

The continued pain in Lysandra's hand rendered her speechless.

"I'm going to kill him," Madeline declared. "And then I'm going to kill her."

"Okay, Mrs. Stone," Dr. Roberts returned to her side. "Try to relax."

"Relax?" she barked, her head ready to twist in a complete circle. "Don't you *dare* tell me to relax when I know my husband is out screwing his big-booty, singing protégé while I'm trying to squeeze out this child alone."

"You're not alone." Lysandra snatched her hand from Madeline's death grip and waved her injured fingers in the air. "I'm here for you, cuz."

Madeline rolled her eyes high, but then another spasm hit. "Drugs," she roared. "I want drugs."

"Mrs. Stone, please relax we're…"

Madeline's snatched the doctor by the neck of his scrubs and jerked him down to eye level. "If you tell me to relax one more *damn* time—"

"Let him go, Maddie," Lysandra urged trying

to pry the doctor loose. "We need him to deliver the baby."

It took a moment, mainly because of the unrelenting pain, but then Madeline released her grip and called on the Almighty to get her through this.

Less than an hour later, a seven pounds and three ounces Ariel Elisa Stone made her grand entrance into the world. The moment Madeline held her bundle of joy, the pain of the last nine hours vanished.

"Hello, Princess," she cooed, pleased to see ten fingers and ten toes. "I've been waiting for you my whole life."

Black, soft curls covered her precious baby girl's head and her eyes were as dark as midnight. Madeline would love this child to the end of time. Convinced Ariel smiled back before releasing a mighty wail, Madeline rode a wave of pride and contentment until her eyelids grew heavy.

Hours later, Madeline woke with a throbbing pain that covered one side of her body. She groaned, shifted and then regretted the action when the pain spread.

"Oh, Maddie. You're awake."

Madeline recognized Lysandra's voice but

didn't understand why it sounded like she was crying.

Something is wrong with the baby.

Her eyes flew open in search of Lysandra and found her petite cousin sobbing next to Madeline's bejeweled mother, Cecelia.

Again, Madeline pushed the pain aside and sat straight up in bed. "Lysandra, what is it? Why are you crying? Where's my baby?"

Lysandra lifted her head and her large brown eyes swam in a large pool of tears. "T-the baby is fine." She sniffed and dropped her gaze again. Her entire five-foot-two-inches body trembled.

Madeline stared, confused. Her cousin must be lying. Lysandra always was a lousy liar. She picked up the red nurse's button and punched it repeatedly.

"What has happened? Why are you crying?" She stabbed the button again.

"May I help you?" A nurse's voice filtered through the intercom.

"I want my baby," Madeline demanded hysterically.

"Never mind, nurse," her mother interrupted in a cool, even voice.

"No," Madeline barked. "I want to see my baby!"

Lysandra shook her head. "It's not the baby," she said again, trying to pry the nurse's button from Madeline's fierce grip between sobs.

"You're lying," Madeline said.

More tears spilled from Lysandra's sad brown eyes. "No, Maddie, I'm not. I-it's Russell."

Madeline stopped struggling and Lysandra successfully pried the nurse's button from her hand. It didn't matter because two nurses rushed into the room wild-eyed.

"What's going on?" they asked in unison.

"Russell?" Madeline repeated dumbfounded. "What about him?"

Lysandra's cell phone chirped from the wooden stand next to the bed. Her cousin didn't reach for it.

Madeline looked to her mother, always the calm one during a storm. "What's going on? Just spit it out. What about Russell?"

"They believe he's dead," Cecelia blurted without emotion. "His private plane disappeared somewhere over the Atlantic." She nodded her head toward the television. "It's all over the news."

Madeline followed her gaze to the muted television where a picture of her husband, music mogul, Russell Stone filled the screen. Beneath it, a red caption read: "Plane Crash."

Lysandra shut off her phone while Madeline's hand scrambled around the bed to find the TV remote. In the next second, the blond reporter's voice filled the room.

Mr. Stone who had just acquired his flying license last year is reported to have logged more than three hundred hours of flying time. There is no word as of yet to what may have caused this accident. Some are suggesting pilot error, but those findings will be left to the International Transportation Safety Board to determine.

Madeline hit the mute button. "I-I think I want to be alone for a moment."

Cecelia offered no further words of comfort, but turned toward the door.

Lysandra placed a consoling hand on her shoulder. "Maddie—"

"Please," Madeline added, looking up to Lysandra and then to the two stricken nurses. "I really need to be alone."

The nurses bobbed their heads and ushered out of the room. Lysandra took up the rear but then cast a final glance over her shoulder. "I'll be just outside the door if you need anything."

Lying back against the bed's pillows, Madeline soberly nodded and waited until the door swung closed behind her cousin. Alone, her gaze cut back toward the television.

She folded her arms as Russell's picture enlarged on the screen. A cold bitterness seeped into every pore of her body. No longer would she have to bear the humiliation of Russell's long string of affairs or pretend to be happy in a loveless marriage.

She was free.

She was rich.

She was happy.

A hard smile curved the corners of her lips. "Good riddance!"

Chapter 1

Six years later...

"**M**other, I'm *never* getting married again," Madeline vowed with a roll of her eyes. "Now, will you just drop it?"

Cecelia Murray-Anderson-Farris-and a few more hyphenated names that currently ended at Howard—gave her daughter an arctic smile while she reached for her glass of wine. "Don't be silly, child. Of course you'll remarry. You're too beautiful to waste away on the shelf. We both are." She looped a lock of hair behind her ears to give anyone who was looking, and there were quite a few, a good look at the sizable diamond-studded earrings she wore.

Madeline sighed instead of laughed even though nothing tickled her more than her mother's *bougie* vanity.

"Don't give me that look, little girl," Cecelia snapped, reading her daughter like the open book she was. "With careful selection, marriage is nothing more than business contract and transaction. Men want something nice and pretty on their arms and a brat or two until the next showroom model turns eighteen. We simply provide a service. Nothing more," she said.

"That might have been so once upon a time," Madeline replied, "but I'm officially retired. Russell left me and the kids more than I'll ever need."

"There's no such thing as enough," her mother scolded without missing a beat. Cecelia's disappointment in Madeline radiated from her body like a nuclear missile. Another sip of her wine and then, "You can't tell me this little hobby of yours isn't going to cost a pretty penny, possibly even put your whole nest egg at risk?"

Hobby. Madeline chomped down her salad so hard her teeth rattled.

"Now, don't get me wrong—" Cecelia smiled, sensing she'd hit a nerve "—I've always thought you had talent…but the fashion industry is like diving into a pool of piranhas. Why risk everything for a…a—"

"A dream?" Madeline supplied, her anger festering. "You ask why and I ask why not?" She leaned forward in her chair to hiss, "Pardon me if I want to be more than just a pretty face on some rich man's arm."

Cecelia arched one delicately groomed eyebrow in reprimand at Madeline's tone.

Chastised, Madeline cleared her throat and apologized.

Silent, her mother sipped her wine while she stared at her.

Madeline shifted in her seat until she couldn't stand it anymore. "I appreciate everything you've taught me, Mother."

"Apparently not," Cecelia seethed. "But children have been known to rebel since the dawn of time. I guess you're entitled to your first temper-tantrum."

Madeline longed to remind her mother that at

thirty-one she was hardly a child. To do so would have been just as effective as trying to kill a lion with a fly swatter.

"Do your little fashion line," her mother said. "And when you lose your butt, as well as your children's financial security, don't say I didn't warn you."

"I knew I could count on you for your support."

Her mother rolled her eyes at the barb. "You know, it scares me how alike we are," she said.

Madeline nearly choked on her meal. She was *not* like her mother. She'd gone through great pains to make sure of that.

"Instead of fashion, I wanted to dabble in acting."

"Really?" Madeline questioned, surprised.

"What? You think you're the only one who can dream?"

"No. It's just… Well, what happened?"

Cecelia lowered her fork, having already digested her maximum allowance of six bites of food. She shrugged indifferently. "I was nineteen, thinking I knew better than my mother and struck out for the bright lights of Hollywood. There were more rich men interested in casting me on a couch than any film projects. I lasted

six months, but managed to snag an engage-
ment from an up-and-coming director. Of
course, he died two months later from a drug
overdose, but he came so close to being my second husband," she said.

Madeline just shook her head. Her mother was
a deep well of amazing stories. Getting an
accurate count of Cecelia's husbands was just as
hard as discovering her true age.

"Six months," Cecelia said after another sip of
her wine. "Six months and you'll be running back
to me with your tail tucked between your legs."

Madeline remained silent, praying that their
weekly lunch date neared its end. "Are you coming
to Russ and Ariel's Thanksgiving school play?"

Cecelia shuddered. No doubt the idea of spend-
ing an evening watching a bunch of tone-deaf
children singing holiday tunes would be just as
horrific as buying her winter wardrobe at Wal-
Mart.

"Maybe next time," she said with a painted on
smile, and reached for her clutch bag. "I almost
forgot. Guess who I saw the other day."

"I give up. Who?" Madeline also reached for
her purse.

"Toby McDaniel."

The groan was out of her mouth before she could think, and Cecelia's eyes narrowed to half their size. "He's a good catch."

"Mother, I'm not interested."

"Made number forty-three on Forbes's richest entertainers."

"Then you take him," Madeline snapped. "I told you. I'm *not* getting married again."

"He likes you. He makes a point of asking about you every time I see him," Cecelia said.

"That's because he gets off thinking he can have something, or someone, that used to belong to Russell. You remember how competitive those two were."

"Who care's about why? He's loaded."

"My answer is still 'no.' And if by some strange miracle I did decide to get married again, the last thing I'd do was marry a man who reminded me of Russell Stone."

Hip-hop and fashion mogul, Christopher Stone nursed his third drink before noon. Some people needed a bowl of Wheaties, he needed a half a bottle of Crown Royal to get the creative juices flowing. In the evening time, his addictions required something much stronger.

He didn't care. He welcomed anything that numbed his emotions. The direct line on his office phone rang and despite his sluggish thoughts, his intuition told him the unwanted caller was his wife…or his new gold-digging playmate he'd met down in Atlanta last weekend.

Either one, undoubtedly, was calling for money.

Christopher drew a deep breath and picked up before the call went to voice mail. "Stone," he said.

"Christopher Stone?" a man asked.

"Who else?" Christopher snapped, annoyed. What idiot didn't know his baby brother has been missing for six years? Missing, *not* dead, he emphasized. Russell was too good a pilot to go down in a storm *and* his body had never been found. In Christopher's book, that left the playing field wide-open.

"Sorry, Mr. Stone," the unidentified caller said in an irritating gravel. "I wanted to make sure I was talking to the right man."

"Talking or wasting my time?" Christopher drained the rest of his drink. "State your business. I'm a busy man."

"Terry Shaw, private detective. We met about five years ago?"

Silence crackled over the line.

"You hired me to look for your brother," Shaw went on.

Straightening in his chair, Christopher's alcohol-induced fog lifted. "What you got? You found something?" No, he didn't recall meeting the investigator. He'd hired so many, but if there'd been some break in the case, if Russell had been found...

"We've found, my assistant and I, someone we think you'll want to talk to."

"You think or you know?" he tested, this thread of excitement already shredding. The last thing he needed was another private dick peddling false hope. It was painful enough getting rid of the last one that came snooping around last year.

Money brought out the worst in people and the ten million dollar reward he'd advertised for information that led to his brother's body or whereabouts had brought out every con artist and flimflam man east of the Mississippi.

Russell Stone sightings were only topped, narrowly, by sightings of Elvis Presley. Witnesses claimed to have spotted Russell in Manhattan, Albuquerque and even Kalamazoo. It all amounted to a pathetic game of 'Where in the world is Carmen Sandiego?' The wasted money wasn't important, but the time and pain had slowly transformed Christopher into a bitter man.

A man, most of the time, he didn't recognize.

"I know, Mr. Stone. I'd like to set a meeting up with you."

Another wave of silence buzzed over the line while Christopher weighed whether he could ride another roller coaster of emotions that would eventually end in disappointment.

"Mr. Stone?"

Christopher sighed and reached for the bottle of whiskey again. "Yes, yes. When do you want to come in?"

"I can be on a plane first thing in the morning and in your office—say, about eleven?"

"Tomorrow is Thanksgiving. I won't be in the office, but you can swing by my house," he said, certain that it wouldn't take more than a few minutes to deal with Mr. Shaw. What difference did it make? The guy would, undoubtedly, be another waste of time.

Chapter 2

"We're going to be rich!" Denitra Bell shouted, and popped the cork on a bottle of cheap champagne, laughing as it bubbled and gushed all over their suite's carpet. "Ten million dollars."

Terry Shaw stretched out across the king-size bed wishing it were filled with his pending reward money. The first thing he was going to spend his riches on was beachfront property in South Miami.

"Whoo, baby. Can you believe it?" Denitra poured two flutes with champagne and joined him at the bed. After he took his glass, she climbed up and cradled his hips in her black, spandex mini-skirt. No panties. "Now, we can definitely afford to get married."

Funny, how some words have the effect of an ice-cube shower.

Denitra undoubtedly felt his hard-on disappear. "What? We are still going to get married, right?"

"Of course we are, darling," Terry lied, slick as a can of oil. Why in the hell should he split ten million dollars with a woman who was just barely old enough to vote? "As soon as Christopher Stone cuts that check, I'll marry you anywhere you want any time you want."

With a smile, Denitra used one hand to slip out of her red, tube top and blinded him with two round, gravity-defying breasts.

Salivating, Terry poured his flute of champagne over her jutting nipples and enjoyed her musical laughter as he pulled her wet body toward him. In no time, she was squirming and his erection returned to full salute. What the hell? After tomorrow he would be a rich man and he could and would replace Denitra with a bevy of barely legal beauties. *Thank you, Russell Stone.*

* * *

After the horrible lunch with her mother, Madeline returned to her office where her team of designers buzzed around her like bees. Her head wasn't in the right place to make so many decisions and it wasn't long before she was irritable and snapping at everyone in a fifty-foot radius. She had hoped for a light workload this week, with the holiday and all. She'd even planned to cook Thanksgiving dinner this year, of course, with the aid of the best cookbooks. But all her planning had been for nothing. She wouldn't have time to cook. It was starting to look like she and the kids were doomed to celebrate another Thanksgiving dinner with her ex-brother-in-law, Christopher, and his divalicious wife, Tiffani.

Not that she didn't like Christopher and Tiffani—well, she didn't—but they were still family to her children. Even so, Christopher nearly suffocated her with dredging up memories and obligatory viewing of aging pictures of her deceased husband.

In the end, the Thanksgiving and Christmas holidays felt like one long memorial to Russell Stone. The first two years after Russell's disappearance were understandable. Without a body, the Stones were denied closure, turning Christopher into a mere shadow of himself.

Frankly, Madeline wished he would just get over it. Lord knew she had.

Christopher and Russell were more than brothers, they were best friends. They were a rare breed of affluent African American men—born with silver spoons in their mouths. And they made sure everyone knew it. Their arrogance barely eclipsed their greed and ambition to rule the hip-hop scene. Just the kind of men that easily won Cecelia's stamp of approval.

At twenty, Madeline was Cecelia's mini me with a mind and body built to broker the best marriage deal she could find. While Christopher was her first choice, it was playboy Russell who'd latched on to her and popped a five-carat Harry Winston diamond ring on her hand in less than three months.

So, yes. Once upon a time, Madeline was a gold digger. And a damn good one. But Mother hadn't prepared her for heartbreak and an iron-clad prenuptial agreement that proved Russell Stone was no dummy. The damn thing even prevented her from cashing in through divorce after his numerous infidelities. Russell was habitually unfaithful. He'd had affairs with anyone including the maid, the nanny, his secretary, groupies and desperate starlets dying to break into the industry.

The only way Madeline could cash in was through his unlikely death. Now, she was a $300 million woman and half owner of Stone Cold Records. Christopher had hoped that she would be more of a silent partner, but Madeline had been about as quiet as a bull in a china store.

She made no apologies for her bitchiness. And as long as she garnered results and more importantly produced a profit, no one else complained. At least not to her face.

E-mailing, texting, phone calls, faxing, the rest of the business day passed in a blur.

Lysandra poked her head into her office in the late afternoon. "Are you ready?"

Madeline frowned, glanced at her watch and groaned. "Damn it. I haven't had a chance to sign off on Godfrey's last alterations."

"It can wait until Monday." Lysandra waltzed into the room, her small frame buried beneath a heavy, black wool coat. "We have to go now if we're going to make it before the curtain goes up."

That's all it took for Madeline to pop out her seat and reach for her coat. "Did you bring a camera?"

"Check."

"Camcorder?"

"Check."

"Ooh, I can't wait to see my babies on that stage. They're going to be the stars of the show."

"As much as a turkey and an Indian Chief can be, I suppose," Lysandra said, and chuckled.

"Laugh now. But in a few years when Ariel is accepting her Oscar, don't say I didn't tell you so."

"I thought she was going to be a famous ballerina?" Lysandra asked, marching behind Madeline toward the elevator bay.

"That, too."

"Marine biologist?"

"My babies are going to be whatever they want to be; whatever they set their minds to. Especially Ariel. The last thing I want her to do is think she's only good for arm candy."

They stepped into the elevator. "Then you better keep her away from her grandmother."

"Check."

What seemed like a lifetime later, Madeline and Lysandra arrived at Russ and Ariel's private school and literally had to run in high-heeled pumps to the theater. Madeline would never forgive herself if she missed Ariel's debut.

As luck would have it, whether bad or good she wasn't sure, Christopher and Tiffani sat front and center, reserving two seats for Madeline and Lysandra. A couple of nods in greeting and Principal Ayers took the stage and welcomed the parents of her students.

Minutes later, Madeline's heart swelled when her handsome, eight-year-old son took the stage to knock on the Pilgrim's door for the nation's first Thanksgiving dinner. True, Russ was a carbon copy of his father as far as features went. He had a strong jawline, two deep dimples and intense, rich, sable eyes that mesmerized, as well as charmed.

At home, the phone rang off the hook with little girls wanting Russ to be their little boyfriend. And just like his father, Russ pretended to be impervious to it all. But there were traces of Madeline in him, too. Her golden honey coloring, her silky "good hair" and her easy laughter.

"How. We come in peace," Russ thundered across the theater and then ushered his Indian family onto the stage.

Madeline grabbed the camera from Lysandra while her cousin manned the digital camcorder.

Christopher leaned over and whispered, "He's a natural performer. Just like his father," he said.

The last tag, Madeline mouthed along with him in annoyance. If she had anything to do with it, and she did, Russ would *not* be like his father.

Yes, Madeline had married Russell for his wealth, but Russell Stone had been a certifiable asshole. Fun and gregarious with friends but selfish and cruel at home. He'd never hit her, but humiliation was his specialty. Four years of marriage felt like four consecutive life sentences in hell.

On the stage, the moment she'd been waiting for unfolded. Her baby, six-year-old Ariel, gobbled her way to center stage and smiled at the crowd as if they'd all come just to see her.

"Oh, how precious," Lysandra cooed.

Madeline couldn't agree more. Ariel, standing an even three feet tall was an amalgamate of Russell and Madeline. She had his thick coarse hair, her hazel green eyes, slim nose, his dimples and full lips. Her skin tone was lighter than her father's milk chocolate had been, but darker than Madeline's golden yellow.

"Maybe you should see about getting her on *Star Search*," Lysandra whispered, jumping aboard the star-in-training fantasy train.

"I told you she has talent," Madeline said proudly.

An hour later, the curtain lowered and then reopened to a standing ovation. Madeline, along with the rest of the parents waved their children down from the stage so they could receive their much-earned hugs. Ariel flew into her mother's arms while Christopher plucked Russ up and swung him around.

"Mommy, Mommy. Did you see? I remembered all my lines!"

"Yes, baby. I saw." Madeline planted a wet, sloppy kiss against Ariel's face that made her giggle.

"I'm so proud of you, baby," Madeline said.

"I remembered my lines, too," Russ wiggled out of his uncle's arms and rushed over to his mother, as well. "And I had more lines."

"Yes, you did, young man. I'm proud of both of you. What do you say we have pizza for dinner tonight?"

Russ and Ariel's eyes rounded to the size of saucers before they screamed and jumped for joy. Junk food was a rare commodity in Madeline's household.

"Actually, Maddie, I was hoping to take the kids out for ice cream or something."

"It's a bit cold for ice cream, don't you think?"

Christopher's face dropped dramatically. "Yeah, well…I was just wanting to spend some time—"

"Didn't Tiffani tell you? We're coming over tomorrow for Thanksgiving dinner."

He brightened and cast a look to his wife for confirmation. Tiffani didn't bother to hide her boredom with the whole proceedings. Most likely, Christopher dragged his wife from some fancy smancy spa.

Hard to believe she was once one of "them."

"Well, then, I guess we'll see you tomorrow night," Christopher said. He pinched Russ's cheek and tickled Ariel's side. "By the way, some P.I. called. Said he had a lead."

Madeline rolled her eyes. There went her good mood. *Why couldn't he just give it up?*

"You guys, go get your coats," she instructed and watched as they raced back behind the stage.

"I'm sure it's nothing," Christopher assured, guessing her thoughts. "He'll be in and out in ten minutes top."

Then why bother to meet with him? She sighed. "I just don't want this whack-job detective, which I'm sure he is, around the kids. As far as we're concerned Russell is dead."

Chapter 3

As usual he woke with a monstrous headache and cottonmouth, but there was one major difference about today. He was going home.

"Home," he said, trying the word on for size, and then waited for some warm fuzzy feeling to pulse through him.

The feeling never came.

However, there was this indescribable void that was in some ways as painful as his headache. Maybe it was a mistake to go 'home.'

"New York." Those words did evoke a feeling in him—a *bad* feeling.

The phone in his suite rang and his throbbing headache intensified and even spread to the back of his neck. The sun had barely peeked through the windows and these people were already bothering him, he thought to himself for the umpteenth time.

"They are just trying to help," he reminded himself, and reached over for the phone before they came rushing over to pound down his door. "Hello," he said into the receiver.

"Mr. Stone," Shaw greeted, a little too cheerful for this time of morning. "Are you about ready to go? We have an early flight."

"Ready when you are." After a few more pleasantries, he hung up and climbed out of bed, completely clothed. Within the hour, the threesome arrived at the airport, where the hustle and bustle of travelers, public address announcements and the sound of airplanes threatened to split his skull in half.

"Are you sure you don't want to take another look at your file?" Shaw asked while they were tucked neatly in their seats in first class.

He looked down and reached for the manila folder without responding to the question. The first photo was of Beverly and Thomason Stone. It was an old picture, perhaps taken in the seventies, but they were definitely an attractive couple.

They appeared to be a rich couple. However, the photograph failed to trigger any emotion, or any memories in him.

Same thing for the picture of Christopher Stone, his brother. The man who'd put up a ten million-dollar reward for his return. "You say we're in business together?"

"Oh, yes. Several businesses, in fact. You're a *very* rich man."

He looked over at the beady-eyes and yellow teeth of the detective. The man didn't induce trust.

The next picture was an eight by ten glossy of Madeline Stone, his wife. His very beautiful wife had long chestnut curls, golden complexion and hazel green eyes. She looked more like someone out of a fantasy than a living, breathing mortal. Truth be told, she was the main reason he was on this plane.

"Ah, it must be coming back to you now," Shaw said, misreading his stare. "I doubt if I'd be able to forget a woman like that myself."

Denitra delivered a sharp jab into Shaw's side.

"Just like I wouldn't be able to forget you, my love," Shaw recovered, and planted a kiss on his girlfriend's pouting lips.

He just shook his head at the weird couple and turned to the photograph. To his smiling portrait.

No doubt about it. The image smiling back in an expensive suit and dripping in gaudy diamond jewelry was him. The same facial features, coloring, hair and eyes... Well, maybe not the eyes. Not that the color was different or even the shape, but the man in the photograph came across as jovial, cocky.... There was something about the man in the picture that he didn't quite like.

"You say that I've been missing for six years?"

"Yes, sir," Shaw said, slapping him on the back. "Your private plane just crashed over the Atlantic. You were presumed dead."

He shifted away from the detective, uncomfortable in his chair.

"Don't worry about not remembering. The doctors say it's not unusual for people to suppress memories after a tragic experience. But when you do remember, I'm sure that it's going to be one heck of a story," Shaw said.

He nodded and then returned his attention to *his* photograph. A man could change a lot in six years. He wondered if his wife would be pleased or disappointed to see him.

On Thanksgiving morning, it was ten o'clock before Madeline even thought to open her eyes and only then because both Ariel and Russ had piled into the bed with her, urging her to get up.

"All right. I'm awake." She removed her gel eye mask and rolled over to tickle Ariel's sides.

Her daughter squealed and kicked her footie pajama feet in the air. "Mommeee," she squealed between peals of laughter.

Madeline loved how Ariel laughed like Woody Woodpecker and she was absolutely adorable with her bushy hair sticking up all over her head. Russ just shook his head and tossed his ever-present football up in the air.

"What time are we going to Uncle Chris's?" he asked. "We're supposed to watch the game after we eat."

Madeline moaned at the thought of an evening filled with football.

"I guess about noon, sweetie. Did Consuela fix you guys breakfast?"

"Yeah. But we just had cereal," he complained.

She reached over rubbed his low-cropped hair. "That's because you're going to have a big meal at your uncle's."

"You're missing the Macy's day parade on TV, Mom." Ariel bounced over her for the bedroom's remote and pushed the button for the plasma screen to descend from the ceiling. Seconds later, Madeline and her small family were huddled beneath the blankets and watching the various cartoon floats as they made their way down Manhattan's Herald Square.

Last year, she and the kids were part of the crowd, freezing their butts off and struggling to get a good view. They'd even managed to drag Cecelia along, even the older woman had whined and complained the entire time.

It was a horrible experience.

This year when she mentioned going back to the parade, the kids' eyes bulged in terror and then hastily agreed to watch the whole thing on television.

Madeline smiled as she glanced over at her babies. So far, the day was off to a great start.

It was noon before Christopher rolled out of bed. Only then did the wonderful aroma of turkey and stuffing, yams and sweet potato pie waft through his sprawling mansion to his nose. A great perk for a man of his means was the ability to hire professional chefs and servers to work on the holidays.

It was a good thing because Tiffani couldn't boil water if her life depended on it.

He rolled out of bed and managed to lumber his way to the bathroom where a hot shower failed to wake him completely. While toweling off, he debated whether to fix a stiff drink, or a piping hot pot of black coffee.

His niece and nephew were coming over after all.

In the end, he settled for both. He made himself coffee spiked with a little something extra.

"God, is it really time for the holidays?" Tiffani complained, dragging her lazy butt out of bed an hour later. "It seems like we just went through all this a week ago."

"It was a quick year," Christopher agreed, watching her traipse naked to the shower. "Are your parents still coming?"

"Yeah. They'll be here around two."

Christopher rolled his eyes. The only word to describe Tiffani's parents was...*ghetto.*

Her father, Cletus, an earsplitting barbeque king from the deepest south of Alabama had the unnerving habit of chewing toothpicks and calling everyone "boy." His mother-in-law, Ruby Jean, ran a hair salon who's secret weapon, judging by her own hairstyles, was globs of hair gel and finger waves.

"Should be another interesting holiday," he said out loud.

At exactly two o'clock family and friends began arriving at the gate. Christopher's special coffee gave him the much-needed alcoholic buzz he needed while he joked and greeted everyone in his bulky Cliff Huxtable-like sweater and unlit cigar.

He didn't truly come alive until his nephew, Russ, showed up with his football. It took very little coaxing to get Russ to toss a few in the backyard, though Christopher could tell by Madeline's dour expression that she didn't approve of them growing so close.

A lot of times, he pretended not to know why she didn't like him, and the times that he couldn't pretend, he just wished that she would get over herself. It wasn't his fault that Russell was a playboy, a daredevil and a not-so-great father. Russell was his own man and made his own decisions.

In his humble opinion, Madeline was mad because she couldn't change Russell. That was what most women tried to do once the ring was around their fingers.

"You guys don't play out there too long. Dinner is going to be served soon," Madeline said, her eyes locked on Russ.

His nephew bobbed his head, but was out the door before she could think up something else to say.

"Lighten up, Maddie," Christopher said, trailing Russ. "He's with me."

"That's what worries me," she said sadly.

An hour later, Thanksgiving dinner was finally laid out like a humongous buffet for the Stones and their closest friends. Christopher, as man of the house, clasped Tiffani's and his father-in-law's hands to lead the group in prayer.

"Thank you, Lord, for this meal that we're about to receive. Thank you for Your blessings of abundance. For those who could not be with us here today…"

Madeline popped open one eye and tried her best to smite Christopher with an evil glare. Just let it go.

"…we hope they are in Thy loving care," Christopher added.

The doorbell jingled and mercifully broke the sober mood Christopher cast. Given the way he'd been swaying on his feet all afternoon, Madeline guessed he was still hitting the booze a little too hard.

Coleman, the butler, a silver-woolen haired gentleman stood at the dining-room entryway with wide dilated eyes. "Er, umm."

Everyone frowned at the man.

"Yes, what is it, Coleman?" Christopher asked. "You look as though you've seen a ghost."

"I think I have, sir."

"What?"

Coleman cleared his throat. "A Mr. Shaw is here to see you and—"

"Who? Oh, yes, the private investigator." Christopher sighed.

"Umm, he brought someone with him. Uh, I believe..."

"Hello, everyone," a short stranger burst into the room.

Madeline stood to remind Christopher to conduct whatever business this man may have with him somewhere in private.

"No, no. Please, everyone, sit down," Shaw instructed. "I didn't mean to disturb Thanksgiving dinner. I just merely wanted to return something that belongs to you." He turned and waved someone forward. "C'mon on in here," the beaming P.I. said.

"Chris," Madeline hissed, but in the next instant,

words died on her lips when a bearded and mustached Russell Stone stepped into the room.

Forty people made a collective gasp. Chairs screeched as dinner guests jumped to their feet.

Russell's eyes zeroed in on his beautiful wife. "Hello, Madeline," he said.

Madeline fainted.

Chapter 4

"Someone call a doctor!"

"It's Thanksgiving. Where are we going to find a doctor to make a house call?"

Madeline wasn't sure, but she was almost certain the last exasperated remark had come from Tiffani.

"Wait. Look, I think she's coming around," someone said."

Moaning, Madeline pried open her eyes, but all she managed was a few millimeters when an explosion of pain forced her to close them again.

"Is she all right?"

That voice. It couldn't be.

No one answered the question, which led Madeline to believe that maybe she'd imagine it. Imagined Russell walking into the dining room as though he'd merely been gone on a fishing trip.

She opened her eyes again, this time forcing them as wide as she could manage. And sure enough she was staring straight into familiar inky black pools of concern.

"It's is you. I didn't dream…" She reached out a hand and winced when she met warm flesh. He was real.

Russell smiled tenderly. "I'm sorry. I didn't mean to alarm you."

Her shock gave way to anger and she whipped her hand hard across his perfectly chiseled features and relished the way his head snapped back. "How dare you?" She jumped up from the leather couch to see that someone had transported her to Christopher's private study. "What is this, some kind of joke?"

Madeline's chest heaved as the first waves of hysteria crashed to shore. "Christopher, are you behind this?"

When her gaze sliced toward her former

brother-in-law, she found most of the color had drained from his face and he'd ditched glasses to drink his beloved Crown Royal straight from the bottle.

Shaw stepped forward and flashed everyone his yellow-toothed smile. "I assure you, this is no joke. This is your long lost husband, Mrs. Stone."

"That's impossible," Madeline said, clinging to denial. "Russell died in a plane crash."

"I'm sure I don't have to remind you his body was never found."

"So what? You're telling me he washed ashore on some desolate island with his bimbo mistress and they've been playing Tarzan and Jane for the past six years?"

Russell stepped back from her obvious hostility.

"Uh, Nova Scotia," Shaw amended. "And there were no signs of the bimbo mistress."

Madeline settled a hand on her hip in annoyance at the short man. "What are you—his publicist? How come he can't talk for himself?"

"Well, there's the slight hiccup," Shaw said, stepping forward. "Seems Mr. Stone here is suffering from amnesia."

"What?" Christopher and Tiffani asked at the same time.

"Oh, give me a break. No one ever has amnesia. That stuff only happens in soap operas. Christopher, this man is trying to take us for a pair of fools. He probably hired some actor and gave him an expensive face job," Madeline said.

"Look, obviously coming here was a mistake," the Russell clone said quietly.

"What was your first clue, Einstein?" Madeline challenged.

"All right. Settle down, Maddie." Christopher finally broke away from his wife's side and approached the imposter. "Of course, tests will need to be done first." He squinted and studied the man's features. "If this is a face job, it's one of the best I've ever seen." He cast a glance over at Madeline. "But how do you explain the voice? I know Russell's voice when I hear it."

She did, too. The realization forced her to swallow a chunk of doubt and look at the man in a different light. Finally, she approached, as well, and looked for any telltale signs in the beard and woolly hair that would give the imposter away.

There wasn't a single one.

"No offense, but this is a little too weird for me," Russell said, stepping back.

A tear trickled down Christopher's face before he stretched out his arms and threw them around the man. "Welcome home, Russell!"

Stunned, Russell awkwardly hugged the man back, but his gaze returned to Madeline. The rage in her hazel-green eyes made her look like an angry goddess. The imagery fascinated him.

"Well, I'm not biting." Madeline walked over and snatched the booze out of Christopher's hand. "I need a drink."

"What are we going to say to all those people out there?" Tiffani questioned, hanging back from Russell.

"We're going to tell them that my brother has returned home." Christopher pulled out his brother's embrace to take another good look. "I know my brother when I see him."

Shaw clapped and rubbed his hands together. "There is still the issue of the reward money."

Madeline groaned and rolled her eyes. "Nothing until a blood test comes back. I mean that."

"Need I remind you that I'm the one who put up the reward money?" Christopher asked. "You never believed he was alive."

Madeline caught the stab of hurt in Russell's expression before she could look away. "Waste your money if you want to," she said, splashing out her drink. "Just keep him the hell away from me and my kids."

"You mean, his kids, don't you?"

"Kids?" Russell looked to Shaw.

The short man shrugged his shoulders. "Sorry, I didn't have any pictures of them to show you, but, uh, you have one boy and one girl."

"How old are they?"

"Like you care," Madeline snapped, and tossed back the amber liquid like a sailor.

"Why wouldn't I care?" Russell asked. He watched as the storm darkened in her eyes, but he trudged on. "Look, whatever differences we might have had in the past, I'm sure it's still no reason to try to keep me from my children."

"*Your* children? It takes more than being a sperm donor to be a real father."

He flinched.

"Maddie, please," Christopher intervened. "The man says he's suffering from—"

"Amnesia. Yeah, I heard," Madeline said.

"Then you know Russell is in no position to defend himself from your vicious attacks," Christopher said.

"Vicious? Need I remind *you* that I was up in

the hospital having his child when he disappeared with that—"

"Again. We don't know what happened that night his plane…" Christopher swallowed and then glanced back to his brother. "It had to have been awful to sustain this sort of trauma for this long."

Madeline rolled her eyes and splashed another inch of whiskey into her glass. "Let's not forget how convenient it is for him to have lost his memory."

"I think it's wonderful," Tiffani piped up.

"You would."

"Baby, you always knew he was alive out there somewhere. You never gave up hope," Tiffani said, sucking up to Christopher.

Put a sock in it. Madeline thought she might begin to heave at any moment.

Christopher proudly puffed up his chest. "I did believe. As close as we've always been I just knew you were out there somewhere."

Madeline washed down the rest of her second drink and headed toward the door.

"Where are you going?" Christopher asked before she reached for the doorknob.

"Home. I've had about enough of this bs."

"Aren't you going to bring the children in here so they can see their father?"

"I certainly am not. We're leaving," she decided.

"Aren't you forgetting something?" Tiffani crossed her arms while holding on to her smug smile. "Your husband? I believe it's his house. And after the blood test, don't stray too far from the phone, the insurance companies will probably want to talk to you."

Madeline nearly wobbled out of her pumps.

Tiffani sauntered up behind her like a lioness closing in on her prey. "If memory serves me correctly you have a lot to lose if he really is Russell. The house, the cars, the money. And no money means no fashion line," Tiffani taunted.

Tiffani's words were like a flurry of surprise left hooks. Madeline tossed a look over her shoulder at her alleged husband. The faker still wore a deer-caught-in-headlights look in his eyes.

"You know. I'm starting to believe you just might be Russell. You always have had an uncanny way of ruining my life," she said as she jerked open the door and stormed out.

Everyone jumped when the door slammed behind her.

"Wow," Shaw said. "She's really a firecracker."

He moved over to Russell and slapped him hard on the back. "Sounds like you were really an asshole."

"Aw. Don't let her worry you," Christopher said, as he came to stand beside Russell. "She's no Girl Scout. Trust me. Tiffani called it right. She's probably worried about losing her money—or rather your money. If you are Russell, my advice is to find a good lawyer, file for divorce and hope that she doesn't beat you to it." He laughed.

Russell shook his head. "She's hurt and it sounds like it's my fault."

The room fell silent.

"Is there anyway I can...see my children?"

"Sure, sure. Wait until you see how much Russ has grown. I tell you, everyone says he's the spitting image of you." Christopher hooked an arm around his brother's neck and led him toward the door.

"Wait. I just want to see them...from a distance. I don't want to upset Madeline any more than she already is. At least not until the test comes back."

"Hey, I already know you're my brother. I'd know you anywhere," Christopher said.

Russell pulled out of his embrace. "But I don't

know you." The moment the words where out of his mouth he regretted them. Christopher's pain was raw and open for anyone to see. "I'm sorry, but I just don't remember any of you."

After a brief silence, Christopher's magnanimous smile returned. "You will. I'm certain of it."

Russell wanted to believe him…

It was hard to dispute he wasn't who they claimed he was, when photos of him sat on nearly every shelf in the house. He followed his brother out onto the office balcony and he'd just caught glimpse of the top of a little girl's head before she climbed into the back of a large silver SUV.

Madeline leaned over, probably to connect the child's seat belt before she quickly slammed the door. After she rushed to the driver's side, she glanced back at the house and spotted Russell.

Despite the distance between them, their eyes locked. His wife's warning to stay away pulsed across the cold fall night as if she had shouted the words at him.

But if the blood test proved he was Russell Stone she might as well get used to him. Because, there was no way he was going to stay away from his wife, or his kids. No way at all.

Chapter 5

"Mommy, was that man really our daddy?" Ariel asked after twenty minutes of silence.

Madeline started to answer with an emphatic "no," but what if the blood test made her out to be a liar? What then? "I don't know, baby," she settled on saying.

"You mean, he could be?" Russ questioned with simple caution. "He looks like him," the little boy said.

"Yes, baby. I know he does." *And he sounds like him, too.*

"Well, where has he been?" Ariel asked. "Why are we going home?"

"How come he's not coming home with us?" Russ inquired. "Did you say something to make him mad?"

"What?" Madeline glanced up into her rearview mirror to seek her son's gaze. "What makes you think I would say something to make him mad?"

Russ lowered his eyes and shrugged.

Madeline returned her attention to the road, stinging from her son's words.

"How come we didn't get a chance to talk to him?" Russ questioned.

"Because…"

"Because why?"

"Just because." She could think of nothing better to say.

"That's no reason," Russ mumbled.

This was exactly what she wanted to avoid.

Ariel started sniffing and Madeline now searched for her in the rearview mirror. "Baby, what's wrong?"

"I want to talk to my daddy," she said between whimpers.

Damn it. Madeline released a long breath and

fought back tears. How in the hell was she supposed to fix this?

She couldn't. In the end, she just had to be the bad mommy. Thanksgiving was ruined because of her. Her children were being denied their father because of her.

The children fussed the rest of the way home. They fussed during their baths and were still fussing when she tucked them into bed. When she finally pried herself away from their inquiring minds she made her way down to the bar and poured herself stiff drink.

What was she going to do if the blood test proved this man was indeed her husband? She took a healthy gulp of her rum and coke. Tiffani was right. His resurrection would reinstate that damn prenuptial agreement. It could undo all she has done in the past six years.

Gulp.

The insurance companies would want their money back.

Gulp.

She would lose her partnership in Stone Cold Records and the fashion line. Not to mention her clothing line would be in jeopardy.

She poured another drink. Why not? Her world

was crumbling in around her. *It's not him. It can't be.*

Tears glossed her eyes as she clung ferociously to denial. Could God hate her this much?

She drained her third drink and carried the pity party up to her bedroom. Now that the alcohol had calmed her nerves, it was easier to allow her mind to drift over Russell's grand reappearance.

He'd walked into the dining room with the same kinetic energy he'd always carried. The same walk, the same stance, the same timbre in his voice. Yet, when she came to in Christopher's study and their eyes connected she'd become…aroused? That had never happened before.

Madeline's head rocked back with laughter. This had to be the booze talking. The days of her being attracted to her husband ended right around the time she'd conceived their child. Madeline clearly remembered the day she'd returned home early and interrupted Russell and some wannabe singer in a very private audition.

Hell, they'd only been married a short time. She'd foolishly believed that she could grow to love her husband. And so it hurt her to know that less than six months after the "I dos," Russell had crept outside their bedroom.

Maddie, you can't expect a man like Russell Stone to be monogamous. Yeah, those hoochie mommas may have him some of the time, but you're the one he comes home to. You're the one with the ring around your finger. That was the world according to Cecelia.

Russell's promiscuity shouldn't have hurt, but it did. The day she'd walked down the aisle, she made a vow to make her marriage work. She wasn't going to try and get into some contest with her mother on who could add the most hyphens to their name.

One marriage. One shot.

Then Russell Stone broke her heart because he operated under the same rules as her mother. While her mother was panning for gold he was looking for a golden trophy to sit on his mantle. The truth was Madeline had been bought and paid for. The Winston diamond ring had sealed the deal.

But then she had violated the contract by trying to add love to the deal.

Shaw took center stage and handed Christopher a Canadian newspaper clipping with a picture of a bearded and mustached Russell next to the caption: *Do you know this man?*

"Denitra and I came across this article while visiting some of her relatives a couple of weeks ago."

Mystery man has refused to speak since he was found wandering near Nova Scotia coast. The mysterious man seemed unable to answer the simplest questions about who he is or where he comes from.

Christopher glanced up at his brother, unable to imagine what he must have been through these past years. "What happened?" he couldn't help but ask.

"I don't know," Russell answered truthfully. "I don't know how I got there or even anyone discovering me. I only remember the hospital," he said.

"The hospital?" Christopher turned back to Shaw.

"Yes. An elderly couple noticed him wandering out there and called the authorities. When the authorities were unable to get any answers out of him, he was taken to Queen Elizabeth Hospital. Their social services are the one's who had contacted the newspaper."

"So you don't know where you've been for the past six years?"

Again Russell shook his head. "I've tried to

remember. But every time I do, I suffer severe migraines."

"He also has a lot of old scars on his body," Shaw interjected. "He's been in some type of accident. That's for sure."

Christopher stood. "Show me."

Uncomfortable with so many pointed gazes in his direction, Russell still climbed to his feet and pulled up his shirt. A round of audible gasps surrounded him as they all peered at his battered and scarred body.

"The plane crash," Christopher whispered as he approached and inspected a few jagged scars up close. "Is that how you got those?"

Russell just looked haplessly at his brother. "I don't know. I don't remember."

Christopher nodded, and then broke out with a wide grin. "What's important is you're home now." He wrapped him in another quick embrace."

Russell was overwhelmed.

Once word of his reappearance hit the grapevine, people poured through Christopher's door. There was a constant flow of men and women who claimed to be friends and relatives. They all tried to get him to remember their names and events. They would ask if he remembered where they did so-and-so, or that such-and-such was so funny when he was a child, a teenager, or a grown man who should have known better.

It also surprised him how many women slipped cards into his hands or pockets with suggestions that they could pick up where they'd left off—whatever that was supposed to mean.

But through all the plastic smiles an awkward laughs, his mind kept wandering back to Madeline. The picture in Shaw's file hardly did the woman justice. Now that he'd seen her—touched her, he desperately wanted to remember everything about her.

Somewhere around 2:00 a.m. Christopher finally responded to Russell's visible exhaustion and led him to one of the vacant guestrooms. In his opinion the room was as big as a studio apartment, complete with a king-size, oak bed with gold silk sheets. On the walls, an eclectic mix of African art surrounded him, as well as an impressive flat-screen television.

"I hope the room is satisfactory," Christopher said, carrying Russell's lone, leather duffel bag in behind them.

"It's…" he looked around again "…it's more than satisfactory."

"Good." Christopher set the bag down on the edge of the bed.

The brightness of his 100-Watt smile had remained intense throughout the busy night. Russell wondered if the thing was permanently chiseled on his face. "Well, I, um, better get some sleep," he said when Christopher made no move toward the door.

"Oh, yeah. Right." Christopher walked backward to the door. "I'm sure you're pretty exhausted and, well, I should let you get some rest."

Russell nodded, but Christopher stopped short from backing out the door.

"It's really good…having you home again," Christopher said.

"It's good to be back," he said more out of politeness. "And don't worry," he added, reading Christopher's fear. "I'll be here when you wake up."

Christopher laughed. "I'm gonna hold you to that. Good night."

"'Night."

However, his brother stopped one last time at the door threshold, his smile finally dimmed. "About Madeline…"

Russell glanced up.

"She's just… Well, we can talk about it tomorrow."

Intrigued, Russell asked the question he'd been dying to know. "How did we meet?"

"What—you and Madeline?" Christopher's smile returned.

"Yes." Russell slipped his hands into his pants pockets. "I tried asking Shaw, but he didn't know. Just gave me the date of our wedding."

Christopher drew a deep breath. "I guess you could say I introduced you two."

"Oh?"

He nodded and rubbed at his neck. The smile was gone. "I guess you could also say you sort of stole her right from under my nose."

"I see." Russell's gaze plunged to the hardwood floor. Talk about cramming his foot into his mouth. "We don't have to talk about this now."

"No. It's okay." Christopher's laugh sounded more like a misfired engine. "I probably should be thanking you."

That comment successfully drew Russell's gaze back to his brother. "Why do you say that?"

A shrug and another misfired laugh. "Madeline is…beautiful no doubt. Grade 'A' quality, but, uh…a little hard to manage, if you know what I mean."

"No. I don't think I do," Russell admitted.

"She's sort of a pistol. Strong willed, overly opinionated and just flat out hard to please." Christopher snickered. "And I believe those were your words."

Russell flinched not just because of the cruelty of the words, but because he's supposedly shared such thoughts with his brother. "She said something about…another woman."

"Lola Crowne." Christopher drew a deep breath. "She went down with you…and the plane. You were both presumed dead." He eyed Russell. "You really can't remember anything?"

How many times tonight had he been asked that very question and how many times had he said, "I'm sorry"?

"Don't worry about it," Christopher said, patting Russell's back in an awkward attempt to cheer him up. "I'm sure it'll all come back to you in time." Christopher headed toward the door.

"We were in love though, right? Madeline and I…at least once upon a time?"

This time, Christopher couldn't manage a smile. "I'll see you in the morning." With that, he left the room and closed the door behind him.

For a long while, Russell stood in the middle of the room, staring at the door while a great emptiness engulfed him. He was home, but he felt more lost than ever. At last, he turned and headed to the adjoining bathroom. It was just as lush and extravagant as the bedroom.

Glancing at his reflection was no different than staring into the numerous faces he'd met tonight. He didn't know the man in the mirror.

He stripped and stepped into the shower. After feeling the different pulses from the showerhead, he was quite content to stay in there for a long time. The hot water massaged the tension from his body. As he let his mind wander, he reviewed everything that had happened that day.

Most importantly, he thought about Madeline. He wondered what had happened between him and Madeline. Earlier, he'd thought he would be returning to the arms of a woman who loved him. In reality, nothing could've been further from the truth.

Russell shut off the water and stepped out of the shower. It was hard to argue that he *wasn't* Russell Stone. So many people, so many pictures couldn't be wrong.

Troubled, he toweled off and wiped the steam from the bathroom mirror. As he looked at the unfamiliar man in the reflection, his eyes were drawn to the ugly, jagged scar down the right side of his body. He supposed a plane crash could explain the wound and the many nicks across his arms and legs.

"Russell Stone." He tried the name on for size and even waited for that magical click of recognition. But the click never came.

In bed, Madeline Stone returned to his thoughts. He imagined what it would be like to pull her body into his arms. What did her full lips taste like...feel like?

Chapter 6

Black Friday—the day after Thanksgiving—lived up to its name.

Madeline not only woke to a massive hangover, but also to find Cecelia glowering down at her.

"What's this nonsense all over the news about Russell Stone rising from the dead?"

"A little louder, Mom. I don't think the people down in Florida heard you," Madeline said.

"They don't have to hear me, I'm sure they're getting the news from CNN just like *I* did this morning. Why didn't you call me? Why are you still in bed? It's noon," Cecelia chided.

"What?" Madeline sat up and squinted at the clock on the bedside dresser. "Oh, God. I told the kids I would take them to the mall."

"It's okay. I told them you were sick. They're over at a neighbor's house, doing whatever kids their ages do."

Madeline groaned. "Your parenting skills always dazzle me." She reached for the phone. "Which neighbor?"

"Stop your bitching. I raised you, didn't I?"

Madeline wasn't going to go near that trap with a ten-foot pole.

"They're fine." Cecelia took the phone out of her hand and hung it back up. "Now, I've waited long enough. Tell me what the hell is going on."

"There's nothing to tell. Yesterday at dinner, this detective walks in announcing he'd found Russell and a man looking just like the son-of-a-bitch walked in behind him."

"Well, is it him?"

Madeline didn't want anything to do with that question, either.

"Oh, my God." Cecelia sat down on a corner of the bed. "It is, isn't it?"

"I didn't say that."

Her mother sighed with relief. "Oh, good. Then it isn't him?"

"I didn't say that, either."

"What *are* you saying?"

Madeline threw her legs over the side of the bed and climbed out. "I'm not saying anything." She rubbed at her eyes. "I don't know what I believe."

"Did he at least say where he's been all this time? What about the woman he'd disappeared with? Did he finally get tired of her and leave her on some deserted island somewhere?"

Madeline slowly pivoted back toward the bed. "Wow, Mom. What a big imagination you have."

"What else can I use in a situation like this? How many men do you know that rise from the dead?"

"Good point."

"But that's not the point that really matters. If he's who he says he is what happens with the money?"

"Moooommm."

Cecelia straightened in her sharp Armani suit. "Madeline, I'm being serious. I suggest you do the same. We need a good offensive *and* defense on this one."

"You're into football now?"

"I'm into winning. And you should be, too." Cecelia stood and picked up the empty liquor bottle from the nightstand before her sharp gaze impaled Madeline. "You didn't do anything stupid last night, did you?"

"I'm not ready to deal with this." Turning, Madeline tried to stomp her way to the bathroom, but it was more like a wobbly walk.

Cecelia marched behind her. "You have to deal with this right now. And frankly, either way you look at it, it's best to get on this man's good side," her mother said.

"Easier said than done." Madeline piled her hair on the top of her head and clipped it in place. "We weren't exactly June and Ward Cleaver. Nowhere close. And let's not forget, he disappeared with his 'ho' of the month, Lola." She squeezed toothpaste onto her brush and began scrubbing like she had a vendetta against plaque.

"Oh, God. You're starting to sound like a broken record. Were you not handsomely rewarded for his 'little' indiscretion?"

Madeline spat out the toothpaste. "Now look who sounds like a broken record," Madeline said.

"I wouldn't have to if you'd start paying attention to me. If you wanted loyalty you should have married Christopher. You ignored me and went after the playboy."

"Christopher—loyal? I should be asking you what you've been drinking this morning."

"Fine. At least, he's more discrete. How's that?"

She grudgingly let her mother score a point while she filled her mouth with mouthwash.

"Plus, you made the mistake in thinking you could change Russell Stone."

Damn. She's two for two.

"You are exactly the kind of woman who gives women in our profession a bad name."

"Mom, I'm in a crisis here," Madeline said, hoping to cut off the Gold digger's anthem.

"Right. And I say play it safe. You get more bees with honey."

"I don't want anything to do with him," Madeline said as she headed to the shower.

"It's not what you *want*. It's about what you *need*. You *need* the houses, the cars, the maids—"

"Moooommm."

"All right. You need the financial backing for the fashion line. Once that's launched, and if it's a success, then you could walk away a rich woman on your own merits. If he's who he says he is and if you push him toward a divorce, he could have most, if not all, your assets frozen for God knows how long, and then where will you be?"

The pulsing in Madeline's head accelerated.

Sensing victory, Cecelia's smile bloomed. "Now, why don't you start from the beginning and tell me about this dead man walking and let your mother help you to get through this and to come out a winner."

The phones were ringing off the hook while news vans and helicopters surrounded the Stone estate. So the natural thing for the family to do was to remain walled up in the lavish, two-story mansion. With butlers, maids and cooks, it wasn't the worst place in the world to be stuck. And yet, Russell felt bad for imprisoning everyone there all the same.

Christopher stared out his study's windows toward the iron gate. "You can't blame them," he said, turning and crossing the room to the empty chair across from Russell. "You are a big story."

"I feel more like a freak at the circus."

"Aw." He waved off his concern. "It won't last long. Real news has a life expectancy of four to seven days. The tabloids, however, can and will stretch this baby out a good six months."

"That long?"

"I'm sure even our dogs will be interviewed

before the whole thing is over with." Christopher laughed.

Russell just forced an awkward smile. He grew even more uncomfortable when Christopher's laughter died and he appeared content to just stare at Russell.

"It's really good to have you back home," Christopher said for the hundredth time.

Mercifully, a knock sounded at the door and Coleman, the butler, entered the study.

"Dr. Rountree is here to see you," he said.

"Yes, yes." Christopher clapped and rubbed his hands together. "Send him in." Then to Russell. "It's time to get this show on the road."

Dr. Rountree, a short and robust black man, charged into the room with chunky glasses and a lion's mane of white coarse hair. His gaze immediately fixed on his patient. Then Russell discovered the doctor had a voice that could be undoubtedly heard in every room of the house.

"My God, it is you!" Rountree continued his charge toward Russell. "I didn't want to believe it until I saw with my own eyes. Where have you been, son?"

"In Canada, if you can believe it," Christopher answered for him.

"A private dick, Terry Shaw, found him at hospital in Nova Scotia. Said he barely recognized him with this full beard and moustache. Thing is, he doesn't remember a single thing."

"Amnesia?" Rountree said the word with wide-eyed wonder. "That's a rare thing, indeed, despite what Hollywood would lead you to believe," he added with a laugh that was as loud as a thunderclap.

"Well, I can tell you on this end, it's not exactly a walk in the park," Russell informed him. "As soon as we get the blood test back, I'll at least feel like I'm moving in the right direction." He caught the flash of disappointment in Christopher's face and he went on to amend, "Although everyone has been pretty nice to me…."

"Hell, it looks like this test is just a formality. I've known you since you were born. You and your brother used to gobble up every piece of candy in my office when you came to see me."

Christopher perked up again at Rountree's words. "I told you on the phone it was a miracle."

"That you did," Rountree agreed. "Well, let's get started. The faster we draw the blood and everything, the faster we can get the results back.

Unfortunately because of the holiday, we won't have the results back until Monday. But again, it's just a formality."

Chapter 7

"What if it is him?" Madeline mumbled under her breath. She stared into her vanity mirror almost hoping that her mirror image would supply an answer, but all she received was her own cool, blank stare.

"Frankly, I don't see how it could be," Lysandra said, perched on the edge of Madeline's enormous bed. She had arrived while Madeline showered and Cecelia had quickly filled her in on the details. "Why should we believe it's him?" she continued. "Look how many scams and con artists we've been through in the last six years. Why would this time be any different?"

"I agree," chimed in Cecelia, while she paced around the room. "But there's nothing wrong with playing it safe. It won't take long for the blood test to come back."

Madeline nodded, but she was quickly developing a migraine. This simply couldn't be happening. For six years she had been free from Russell Stone and the idea, however small, of returning to captivity was enough to threaten her sanity.

Madeline took a deep breath and then whispered, "Maybe I should go back."

"Where?" both Cecelia and Lysandra questioned.

"To Christopher's. To take another look. To make sure." Madeline stood from the vanity table and joined her mother in pacing around the room. "I'll go crazy if I stay here, wondering." She stopped pacing. "I can't lose everything I've worked so hard for now. I've come too far. I'm too close to the label's launch."

"If you're going then I'm going with you," Cecelia announced. "I want to see this man for myself."

Madeline groaned.

Lysandra jumped up. "I want to go, too."

"I need one of you to stay here with the children," Madeline said.

"She can do it," Cecelia and Lysandra responded, both pointing to the other.

Madeline turned her imploring eyes toward her cousin. Both knew that it wasn't fair to subject Russ and Ariel to Cecelia's burnt or under-cooked meals and constant nagging.

"Fine," Lysandra relented, plopping back down on the bed. "I'll stay, but I expect a full report on what's going on."

"You got it," Madeline promised. "One way or another, I'm getting to the bottom of this."

Dark sky. Angry clouds. Falling, losing altitude, losing control. Smoke. He could smell smoke.

"Mayday! Mayday!"

A voice, his voice, cried for help. Twisting and clawing, he struggled to fight his way out of the nightmare; however, the more he wrestled the faster he fell.

"We're going down! Dear God, we're going down!"

Suddenly he was plunging out of the sky at an alarming rate. He tried to scream again, but now he couldn't squeeze air through his lungs. Blood rushed and then threatened to burst his eardrums, while every muscle in his body clenched in preparation for the inevitable crash.

A second before impact, Russell's eyes snapped open and his heart leapt at the sight of a lone figure hovering above him. Without thinking, he shot out his hand and gripped the stranger's slim neck. He had every intention of squeezing until the small bones snapped in two, but a woman's husky whimper parted the thick fog, clouding his judgment.

"Rus-sell," the woman gasped, while long, slender fingers raked at his hand. "Please… stop."

"Madeline," he whispered. Recognition snapped into place and his hand dropped away from her neck as though it was a hot poker scorching his skin.

Madeline jetted backward and toppled over the edge of the bed and hit the floor with a loud thump.

"Oh my God, Madeline," Russell rasped, and then rushed out of bed and raced to her side.

Madeline scrambled away from him. "Don't

touch me!" she screeched, her hands covering her bruised neck.

Russell held up his hands so she could see that he meant her no harm.

"You tried to kill me," she accused, her tone unforgiving.

"I was startled. I'm sorry… I didn't know," he apologized. His guilt and his repulsion at what he'd done, what he'd been seconds from doing, ripped at his soul.

Madeline's beautiful eyes blazed with disbelief and mistrust. He could hardly blame her. Reluctantly, he backed away from her. "I'll call for someone to come up and help you," he whispered in remorse, and turned to reach for the phone.

"No. Don't," Madeline barked.

Surprised by the command, Russell turned and stared at his beautiful wife. His wife, he thought incredulously. Since when did he start believing that she truly belonged to him?

"It's okay," she assured in a strained whisper. "I'm okay." She climbed up on her visibly shaking legs. "It looked like you were having a bad dream."

Was he?

"What were you dreaming about?" she asked, eyeing him suspiciously.

He stared back at her, his mind a blank. "I don't remember," he said. It was only partly true, but until he could make sense of everything, he elected to keep his disturbing dreams, or rather nightmares, to himself.

It didn't matter. The look on Madeline's face clearly said that she didn't believe him. Backing away, she said, "It was a mistake to come back here." She pivoted on her black heels, but didn't walk far.

"Then why did you?" he asked, his curiosity getting the best of him. "You made it pretty clear last night you hate my guts."

She stood frozen with her back toward him. "I never said that."

"You didn't have to."

Madeline straightened her shoulders and lifted her head before she dared turn and face him again. "Are you really my husband?"

Russell met her leveled gaze with one of his own. "I don't know. I came here hoping that you could tell me."

Madeline stared into the man's liquid black orbs with a racing heart and a million butterflies fluttering in her stomach—neither of which had anything to do with fear, but had everything to do with a burning attraction. "You're not my husband," she said, forcing each word out of her mouth. At the moment, she believed it. Her husband had never affected her like this.

Russell dropped his gaze to stare at a vacant spot on the floor. "Do you believe that, or do you simply want to believe it?"

Their eyes met again, and this time, Madeline felt the acidic burn of rising tears. "I want Russell Stone to remain dead and buried."

He physically flinched from her bitter words and in the next second, his entire posture slumped with disappointment. "Then I hope for your sake that he is."

Guilt stabbed Madeline's heart. She had never seen a man look so remorseful and tortured. The old Russell Stone knew how to stand toe to toe with her and engage in a verbal combat that left everyone in New York with their ears ringing.

That was what she had halfway expected when she raced back to Christopher's. She wanted to scream, rake his eyes out, if need be. But now, she had to fight all that was holy not to take him in her arms and comfort him, tell him that everything was going to be all right.

Even though it was far from the truth.

"Why don't you just go back to wherever you

came from?" she asked as fat drops of tears rolled down her face. Better to get through this ugliness now than to drag it out. She wanted him gone.

While she waited for him to respond, the silence in the room condemned her for being so ruthless. This man may or may not be her husband, but one thing she was certain of, this man was lost.

He was not an actor and he was not faking his amnesia.

"I'll leave," he finally said, and somehow managed to lift his shoulders a few inches. "If and when the blood test proves I'm not Russell Stone."

It was Madeline's turn to be disappointed.

"Do cheer up," Russell said, stepping forward. "The last thing I want to do is hurt you." He cupped her chin between his fingertips, locking their gazes once again. "I do have a confession though," he said.

"What is it?" she asked though she was scared to hear it.

"I hope I am your husband. So I don't have to ask permission to do this."

Before she could react, he leaned forward and planted his pillow-soft lips against hers. She sighed, melting into the kiss and gave no resistance when his hands fell and wrapped around her waist.

He didn't pull her closer, he didn't have to. She willingly pressed her body against his with a carnal lust that shook her very core.

One knock, and then the bedroom door bolted open. "Russell, Madeline is…" Christopher froze just as Madeline and Russell sprang apart.

"Back," Christopher finished his sentence with a lopsided smirk. "Well, well, well. Look who's kissed and made up."

"Go to hell," Madeline said, finally feeling her anger, however misdirected, return. She marched from Russell's side, and breezed past Christopher with a rough bump to his arm.

He laughed in her wake and then turned his amused gaze back toward his brother. "You still got the touch."

Russell flushed with embarrassment. "I think things are looking up."

Christopher just shook his head as he approached. "Let me remind you of something you have obviously forgotten: never underestimate a woman with a plan. And right now, you're all that stands between Madeline and a hell of a lot of money."

Chapter 8

"You kissed him?" Lysandra screeched through the phone. "Are you feeling okay? What possessed you to do something stupid like that?"

"Please," Madeline moaned. "One question at a time. I've obviously misplaced my brain somewhere."

Lysandra fell silent for so long, Madeline had to check whether she was still on the line.

"Yeah, I'm still here. I just don't know what to say. I thought you hated Russell?"

"I did. I do, but…"

"Yes?"

Madeline gave up searching for logic and shrugged against the phone. "I can't explain what happened."

"Well…does this mean that you think he *is* Russell?"

"That's just it, I still don't know."

"Even after kissing him?"

Again, logic escaped her. "Russell has always been a master kisser. It's what made him popular with the ladies."

"Second to his money?"

"I guess it's all relative—but…when I kissed him, it was the same—but totally different. I can't explain it any better than that." *Other than he swept me off my feet.*

Lysandra released a loud sigh. "Well, you set out to discover the truth. I guess this was one way to go about doing it." Silence, and then, "I just wouldn't make kissing him a habit."

Good sound advice. Madeline nodded against the phone.

"Are you still there?" Lysandra asked.

"Yeah, I'm here." Madeline stood from the bed and paced. "It's him," she finally whispered. "No way this guy is an actor. As crazy as his amnesia story is, I think…I believe him."

"That's not good news," Lysandra said.

Madeline stopped pacing and reviewed the kiss in her mind for about the hundredth time in the last ten minutes. What she remembered now and what she tasted then was possibility.

Can a bad boy be reprogrammed?

Madeline laughed at the question. There were way too many women crazy enough to think that changing a man was a possibility. Sure you can get them to take the garbage out every now and then and you're one of the lucky ones if you could train them to keep their clothes off the floor, but change a playboy into husband material?

Been there. Tried that.

"You're right, Lysandra." She nodded. "I need to stay focused. "If he's my husband, I just need to keep the peace until after the fashion line launch. I haven't come this far to lose everything now."

Despite what Shaw thought, Denitra wasn't dumb. In the past twenty-four hours in the Stone estate, she'd experienced a level of luxury she'd never known existed. Why settle for half the reward money when there was obvious so much more available?

The idea of marrying shifty-eyed Shaw became less appealing and the handsome, amnesia gold mine Russell Stone became her new golden ticket—especially since the reunion between him and the missus looked more like the beginnings of a new world war.

However, she was hardly in the same class as Madeline Stone. The woman exuded elegant style.

"Baby, what's wrong?" Shaw finally stopped huffing and puffing above her to actually notice she wasn't participating.

"Actually—" she sighed "—I do have a bit of a headache."

Shaw's three-minute hard-on deflated and Denitra rolled her eyes, as well as her body off their silken-sheeted haven and made a beeline toward the bathroom.

"Hey, what the hell has gotten in to you?" Shaw asked, trailing behind her. "You've been trippin' since we got here."

"Oh, please. You're imaging things." She turned on the shower. "See if you can get me some aspirins or something. We're expected at dinner in a few minutes." Denitra tuned Shaw's babbling out as she assessed her figure in the mirror. She definitely had the figure to capture Russell Stone's attention—now she needed the polish.

Just thinking what she should wear next to men and women who only wore top-of-the-line, designer clothes really did threaten to give her a headache. She wished she could be more like them.

She'd have to learn and learn quickly if she wanted a man like Russell Stone to notice her.

Russell stood before the bathroom mirror and took one last long look at his thick moustache and scruffy beard and then reached for the electric razor Coleman had brought him. At first, he felt like an invalid trying to maneuver the gadget, but within minutes he had the hang of it. When he finished, he roamed his hand across his now smooth skin and finally saw what everyone else did—Russell Stone.

Coleman returned and proved to be one hell of a barber. Dinner didn't call for an Armani suit, but Coleman had selected a black and gray Valentino number that draped his toned six-foot-two physique like an actor on the red carpet.

"Are you pleased, sir?" Coleman asked.

Russell kept turning before the bedroom mirrors, marveling at the transformation.

"Sir?" Coleman prompted again.

"Yes, yes," Russell answered at last. "You did a good job, Coleman."

A smile lit Coleman's eyes, but it didn't touch his lips. Russell found the older gentleman an interesting oddity, but he liked him.

"What time is dinner served again?" Russell asked, eager to see his wife again. *Wife.* When had he accepted that notion as fact? Probably the moment he laid eyes on her and started wishing it to be true.

"Dinner will be served promptly at seven, sir."

"Coleman, it's not necessary to keep calling me 'sir.'"

"Then what shall I call you?" he asked, maintaining his stoic expression.

Silence, and then softly, "Russell. For the time being you can call me Russell."

At last, a smile curved the butler's full lips. "As you wish."

Madeline expected Christopher to host another large dinner, this time for the curious, family and friends who'd missed the main event the night before. Instead, the table was set for seven.

"This should be cozy," Cecelia commented.

"Less company means we'll have more of opportunity to grill this impostor."

Madeline glanced at her overly bejeweled mother. "You think he's a fake?"

"Of course he is. Did you see that disgusting beard and moustache—and those clothes? The horror!"

"Mother—"

"I know what I'm talking about. Good breeding stays in the bones, amnesia or not."

Speechless, Madeline shook her head. She wondered for the umpteenth time why she had invited her mother.

"Where shall we sit?" Cecelia asked.

"Anywhere is fine," Madeline said, drawing back the first chair she approached.

Her mother's hand wrapped around her arm like a steel vise and prevented her from sitting down.

"I want you to sit next to him—*the fraud.*"

Madeline didn't like that idea. Despite her earlier bravado on the phone with Lysandra, she was certain, she needed a bit of distance from Russell in order to think clearly. "That's not necessary, Mother. We're going to be here all weekend. There will be plenty of opportunity to get up close and personal."

"I—"

"I can't see how anyone could forget a house like this," a woman's low husky voice filtered into the dining room seconds before a curvaceous woman wrapped tightly in hooker spandex appeared in the doorway.

Her familiar face teased Madeline's memory and before she had a chance to figure out where she'd seen the girl before the shifty eyed private investigator burst onto the scene. He wrapped his arm around the woman's curvy waist in silent possession. His arm candy looked none too pleased with him or at seeing Madeline.

"Speaking of bad breeding," Cecelia said icily.

"I see you're still here," Madeline said with disdain dripping from her voice.

"Until the check is written." Shaw winked, and then added, "I'm more surprised to see you here. That was quite a performance last night. Very Dynasty-esque."

Madeline clamped her jaw tight until the urge to sock the P.I. in the face passed. It was going to be a long night, she thought.

Cecelia stepped forward to fill the room's sudden silence. "I take it then that you are the man who found this Russell look-alike?"

"He's the genuine article." Shaw dropped his arm from his spandex goddess. "I stake my reputation on it."

Cecelia's eyebrows soared to the middle of her forehead. "Well, excuse me if that doesn't exactly cause me to sleep better at night."

Tiffani and Christopher glided into the dining room next. While Christopher wore a smile to rival the sun, Tiffani looked bored.

"Hello, everyone," Christopher greeted as his eyes scanned the room. "I see that our guest of honor hasn't arrived yet." His gaze settled on Madeline. "Given how chummy you two were this afternoon I thought you would do the honors of escorting him down to dinner."

Shaw was off the hook and Christopher now replaced the punching bag in her mind.

"Again, my apologies for interrupting your afternoon delight."

"What?" Her mother and the spandex queen gasped.

"What's it to you?" Shaw questioned his date.

"Nothing," the woman answered. "I'm surprised is all."

"Nothing happened," Madeline lied.

Suddenly, Russell's smooth baritone floated

into the room. "I thought something happened," he said.

Everyone whipped around and made a collective gasp at the polished GQ ghost of Russell Stone. He stepped through the archway, eyes locked on Madeline.

Everyone, except his wife, crowded around him in approval of his transformation.

Everything about him was exactly the same... except for the eyes. Still a rich sable, but the soul within was damaged. For the first time Madeline wondered what the past six years has been like for him. To be lost. To not know who you were.

Russell smiled.

Madeline smiled back.

Madeline assessed in his low-cropped hair, his creamy milk-chocolate skin, his broad, but lean physique and finally came to terms with the truth—Russell Stone was back. Brick by brick, the walls of her defenses crumpled to the ground. And in that moment, Madeline realized she'd never been more scared in her life.

Chapter 9

A chivalrous Russell pulled out his wife's chair at the dinner table and then smiled at her in a way that made her skin tingle.

"You look lovely this evening," he said quietly by her ear. The sound of his deep voice sent a tingle to each of the nerve endings along her spine.

"You clean up pretty good yourself." Madeline managed to say.

"I was trying to impress you," he said with an adorable crooked grin.

"Mission accomplished." She couldn't bring

herself to admit she missed the scruffy beard and mustache.

Russell winked and then walked to the other side of the table.

Caught blushing like a silly teenager with her first crush, Cecelia leaned toward her and spoke with a note of awe. "I stand corrected. It *is* him."

No, Madeline thought. This was a better version of Russell.

Everyone took their seats, leaving the chair directly across from Madeline free for Russell.

Christopher chuckled and the sound melted the smile off of Madeline's face. When she made a cursory glance around the table, all eyes were on her.

Cecelia leaned over again. "What's wrong with you?"

"Nothing," the whispered lie slipped from her lips. "I was just being…friendly."

The night's menu consisted of Russell's favorite Italian foods—fried calamari as an appetizer, chicken scarpariello for the main course and crème brûlée for dessert.

Madeline suspected the meal was Christopher's attempt to jar some nugget of memory loose in

Russell's head, but Russell just gave the meal a per-functory compliment and returned to gazing at her.

"So when do we get to hear your side of things?" Cecelia asked, her boredom of the idle chatter echoed in her voice. "You don't remember who you are, but what do you remember? There had to be a story before this Bozo—" she indicated Shaw "—popped up and told you who you were. What were you doing?"

"Mother!" Madeline was mortified.

"What? It's a perfectly good question," Cecelia replied.

True, Madeline thought. It was way past time for a more in-depth explanation of Russell's story, but she couldn't halt this newfound protectiveness. "Can't it at least wait until after dinner?"

"It's okay," Russell interrupted the budding argument. "I don't mind answering. I don't have anything to hide."

The table fell silent as all eyes fell on him.

Glancing around, Russell cleared his throat. "Actually, Mrs—?"

Eyes shifted around the table.

"Currently, Ms. Howard. I've had a couple of marriages since the last time I saw you, but if you are whom you claim to be then I'm also your mother-in-law," Cecelia said.

"Ah," Russell said. "I assumed sister-in-law given the striking resemblance."

To everyone's surprise, Cecelia's face blushed a deep burgundy from the compliment. She flashed Russell a genuine smile.

Smug, now that the tables had turned, Madeline leaned toward her mother and asked, "What in the world is wrong with you?"

Cecelia's smile evaporated. "Please do go on with your story…Russell."

Russell set aside his napkin and retold the same story Shaw related the night before.

Denitra took the spotlight with a broad smile. "I was the one who saw the article first. It ran with a grainy black-and-white photo. Despite the beard and the moustache, I knew there was something familiar about the shape of his face," she said.

Cecelia gave the young woman a withering smile. "Very good, dear. You can read."

"Then she brought the article to me," Shaw interrupted. "And I went and checked it out."

Denitra's hands flew to her hips as she glared at her partner. "We went and checked it out," she said.

"Well," Christopher leapt in before the argument escalated. "We're grateful to both of you," he said.

The detective and the tramp clammed up and forced smiles on their faces for their host.

"It's certainly an intriguing story," Cecelia said. "It's just too bad about the amnesia part. It leaves a lot of questions unanswered."

Madeline's gaze dropped to her half-eaten meal.

"You know the answers to more questions than I do," Russell said. "There's nothing I can do about the past, Ms. Howard. All I can do is ask for forgiveness and move on."

Madeline didn't look up, but she felt the weight of his stare. Could she ever forgive him *or* forget about their past? She wrestled with the question while playing with her food. By the time everyone excused themselves from the table, she was no closer to an answer.

Christopher pounded a hand against his brother's back. "What do you say we share a smoke in my study? I just so happen to have a new box of cigars we can share over a nice glass of Brandy."

Russell frowned. "I don't smoke." He thought for a second and then added, "Do I?"

Everyone shared an awkward chuckle, even

Madeline couldn't help but join them. "Another one of your disgusting habits." She regretted the words the moment they flew out of her mouth. "Sorry," she added after a glance at his wounded expression.

"Don't be." He turned to Christopher. "Perhaps another time? I hoped Madeline would join me for a walk outside?"

Again, all eyes shifted in her direction. "Well, I, uh—"

"Would it help if I said 'please'?"

His eyes implored her and more bricks tumbled from her wall of defense. "Sure. Let me just go up and get my jacket." When Madeline left the dining room, Cecelia followed fast on her heel.

"What exactly is your plan?"

"Plan?" She rushed up the stairs, hoping to shake her mother. Of course, she had no such luck.

"Don't play games with me. What are you going to do now that your husband has returned from the dead?"

"There's nothing to do. I'll have to return the life-insurance money and give up my stake in Stone Cold Records and the fashion line."

"Oh, is that all?" Cecelia asked, matching Madeline's tone of nonchalance. "Are you going to divorce him? What about the prenuptial agreement?"

Madeline rolled her eyes as she breezed into the guestroom. "I don't have a firm plan, Mother. I just know I don't want to do anything that may jeopardize *House of Madeline*. The way things are going, the only way to finance the project is with Russell's money. If I was dealing with the old Russell—"

"You wouldn't have a snowball's chance in hell," her mother conceded, and smiled as Madeline slid into her fur coat. "Sounds like a firm plan. I keep telling you we're so much alike."

Madeline froze.

Cecelia sobered. "What?"

"Nothing," Madeline lied, and then marched out of the room.

"Are you sure you don't want me to send someone to act as a bodyguard for you?" Christopher joked while they waited for Madeline. "Your wife has been known to have one heck of a right hook."

"That much I know." Russell rubbed his jaw. "I'm still feeling the one from last night."

Christopher nodded, opened his mouth but then quickly closed it.

"What is it?"

"Huh?"

"There's something you want to tell me," Russell said, observing him. "Tell me."

Christopher glanced toward the empty staircase and then back at his brother. "It's about you and Madeline. I, uh, don't know exactly how to tell you this but, uh…" another glance at the staircase "…before your…accident. Things between you two weren't all that good."

"Yeah. I gathered that was the reason for the right hook last night. That and my…the lady, Ms. Crowne, I crashed with."

"That's just it," Christopher said solemnly. "It wasn't just one lady."

Russell frowned. "What do you mean?"

"I mean…you were known to be quite the ladies' man." He cleared his throat. "We actually have that in common." While Christopher paused to let his words sink in, Madeline appeared at the top of the staircase.

"There were more?" Russell asked.

"We can talk about it later," Christopher promised and then beamed up at Madeline. "That was quick!"

Madeline took one look at Russell's slack jaw and asked, "You can talk about what later?"

"Everything," Christopher supplied. "The business, family, you name it."

Suspicious, her gaze swung between the brothers. Russell looked stricken and had yet to meet her eyes. "Are you all right?" she asked.

"Y-yes," he croaked, and then cleared his throat. "Are you ready?" He reached for the front door. "I'm depending on you to be the guide."

"It's pretty hard to get lost," she said, crossing the threshold and into the cold night. She tugged her collar around her ears and burrowed a portion of her face into the warm Chinchilla. "Maybe this isn't such a good idea. It's freezing out here."

Russell closed the door behind them and surprised her by wrapping an arm around her waist. "I can keep you warm, if you like?"

Madeline's knees buckled as thin white clouds of her frozen breath puffed out in front of her. By some miracle, she found the strength to ease out of his embrace. "I can manage."

An awkward smile wobbled onto Russell's face. "Sorry. I-I…forgive me." He offered his arm. "How about that walk?"

Drawing a deep breath, she slid her arm through his and then led him down the stone porch.

Instantly reminded of their brief courtship, Madeline piled a few more bricks back onto her wall of defense and prepared for anything. Instead, while they walked around the perimeter and entered the Stones' winter garden, Russell remained silent.

Stealing a sideway glance, the man at her side appeared lost in his thoughts as he measured his steps, staring at the ground. Grateful for the opportunity to watch and study him more freely, Madeline failed to find anything amiss in his profile.

"Do I pass inspection?" Russell asked, suddenly.

She jerked her gaze away in embarrassment.

Russell laughed. "It's all right. I'm getting used to being stared at."

Madeline looked at him again. "It's just that it's all so…unbelievable. A miracle, really."

"It's not a good one for you, I take it?"

Should she lie?

"I have to tell you," he said. "I'm not as confident or as certain as everyone else about this whole thing." His gaze returned to the ground. "I feel like a fraud in these clothes."

Madeline continued to silently stumble her emotional labyrinth continued and she chose to remain quiet.

"I want to remember." He turned toward the house. "Heck, who wouldn't want to remember a place like this?"

"Actually, you didn't live here," she said, forgetting her decision to not talk. "Our house is a few minutes north of here."

He turned toward her, his face washed in silver moonlight. Madeline's heart skipped more than a few heartbeats.

"Tell me about it."

"Well," she said, trying unsuccessfully to pull her gaze away. "It's a little bigger than Christopher's place."

"Bigger?" He frowned. "How much room do we need?"

She blinked, once again thrown off guard. "Uh, actually, you and Christopher have always had this sort of competition. You know, houses, cars—"

"Mistresses?"

The rest of Madeline's words died on her tongue.

Russell attempted to smile, but it hung awkwardly on his lips. "Christopher said I stole you from him. Was it because of a burning attraction between us…"

"Or a strategic chess move?" she asked for him.

He nodded.

"Only you can answer that question," she admitted and feared his next question, but it came anyway.

"What was it for you?"

A calculation for the best lucrative marriage edged by a small spark of physical attraction. "It was combination of things."

He nodded but his gaze seared straight through her. "Mind if I ask you a question?"

"You just did."

He finally flashed a genuine smile, however, it didn't stay long. He seemed to struggle with his next question. "Madeline, did you marry me for the money?"

Chapter 10

"What did you tell him?" Lysandra asked, eyes as wide as silver dollars. "C'mon, you've left me hanging for two days. You're killing me. Just tell me!"

Madeline marched across her office to her door and glanced around to make sure no one had overheard her excited cousin. A few curious eyes drifted her way, but the staff had been eyeballing her all morning. Everyone was dying to question her about Russell's miraculous return. *Let them stew.* She closed the door and turned to her cousin. "Keep your voice down."

"Well?" Lysandra persisted. "Don't give me the story in piecemeal. Spit it out."

Madeline crossed her arms, still feeling Friday night's cold chill. "I told him the truth. What else could I do?"

Lysandra dropped into one of the room's empty leather chairs. "You could've lied," she offered weakly. "Have you forgotten what's at stake here?"

Madeline hands exploded up into the air. "How can I with you, Mother and my conscience driving me up the wall every five minutes?"

"Then why in the hell did you tell him the truth?"

"Why lie?" She returned to her cluttered desk, unsure of which pile of sketches, swatches or financial spreadsheets to dive into first. "I married for security and Russell married a trophy wife to produce a couple of kids to carry on the Stone family name. The old Russell understood these things. If I was ever confused, his endless parade of girlfriends quickly put me in my place. You know. You were there."

"And the new Russell?"

He looked crestfallen, Madeline thought, but said, "It doesn't matter."

"But the line—"

"Will be fine," Madeline snapped. "You know

there's still a chance we're dealing with an impostor and in that case we're just spinning our
wheels for nothing," Madeline said to her cousin.

"Do you still believe there's a chance he's an
imposter?"

No.

"I'm saying that we have ten months before we
launch and I'd rather concentrate on that right
now. I'll deal with everything then. When the
blood test results come in. My biggest headache
right now is how to explain all of this to the
children. It's bad enough I kept them out of school
today, but I will have to give them some kind of
explanation."

Lysandra opened her mouth to argue, but Madeline had perfected her mother's highbrow stare and
her cousin exhaled a long breath and then heaved
herself out of the chair. "Fine." She strolled to the
door. "I just hope you know what you're doing."

"Close the door behind you," Madeline ordered. Once alone, she slumped back in her chair
and rolled her eyes toward the ceiling.

Do I know what I'm doing?

Russell couldn't keep Madeline out of his
mind—not that he was trying that hard. He found

everything about her fascinating. She had beauty, brains and, above all else, honesty. When he'd ask whether she married him for money, he fully expected her to be outraged by the question. Then after a brief pause, he wanted her to deny it. But when she calmly told him "yes," he could only respect her.

A knock on his bedroom door jarred him from his thoughts and his shoulders slumped at the prospect of Christopher probing his already taxed brain to force memories into his consciousness that simply eluded him.

"Who is it?" he inquired, crossing to the door.

"Laurell," a woman whispered.

Who? He opened the door and then had to rush backward when the woman's tall willowy frame bolted inside, kicked the door closed with the back of her heel and wrapped her arms around him.

"Oh, baby. I can't believe you've really returned to me."

Before Russell could speak, the strange woman blanketed his face with kisses.

"I was off for the holidays, but when the kitchen staff told me about your return, I cried with joy." She kissed him again and began to pull at his clothes.

"Whoa. Whoa." He grabbed at her arms. "There's has to be some kind of mistake." He tried to push her away, but instead found himself tumbling backward onto the bed.

A devilish grin seized the young woman's face and she dove on top of him. "Don't fight me. It can be just like it used to be. Well, I am married now, but what Henry doesn't know won't hurt him."

What? "Look, lady. There's been some kind of mistake. I'm not who you think I am. I mean, I am...but I'm not."

She stopped, stared at him and then burst out laughing. "Come on. You're not gonna pull that amnesia bit with me, are you?"

He shook his head and struggled for the right words. "I—I'm sorry, but—"

"Well, maybe these will jog your memory." Laurell ripped open her shirt and sent buttons flying in all directions.

Russell's eyes widened at the sight. Two full cantaloupe-size breasts were crammed into a black, lacey bra. A half a second later, she unsnapped the bra by a center clasp and his eyes bulged even wider.

A knock sounded at the door. "Russell?" Christopher inquired through the door.

"Damn!" Laurell bounced off the bed and ran in a complete circle, trying to find a place to hide.

Russell watched the doorknob turn as he stood up from the bed. "Uh, just a minute," he called out in a panic. "I'm not descent."

The door opened. "Why would I care if…?"

An eerie quiet fell over the room, but then it was replaced by Christopher's loud laughter.

"Still got the magic touch, eh, Russell?"

Laurell ducked her head and rushed out of the room.

Christopher held on to his smile as he watched her leave and then turned back to his brother. "I swear, those tits you bought her was one of your best investments."

"Me?"

"When she first came to work here, she was flat as a pancake." Christopher looped an arm around him. "Now they're every man's dream and my Thursday-afternoon pillows."

Russell frowned. "You and she…her and I…?"

"Hey, bro. We share everything," Christopher said, and winked slyly at his brother.

Madeline flashed in his mind and a sudden anger flared in Russell.

"Well, almost everything," Christopher amended

with a hard pat to Russell's back. "Dr. Rountree promised to call within the hour. I had my secretary set up a press conference and—"

"A what?"

"A press conference. The media is hungry for information about you and your story."

"But what if the test results…"

"I don't need a blood test to know you're my brother."

Russell admired Christopher's confidence, but also experienced that overwhelming fear of letting the man down.

"After that, I figured we'd have a car take us over to Stone Cold Records. I'm told the staff is buzzing about your return. How does that sound?"

More people. Russell smiled despite the ball of anxiety curling in the pit of his stomach. He hadn't even had a chance to see his two kids yet. And that was assuming they even were his. Either way, he desperately wished everything and everyone would slow down.

"Well, we can always stop by the label another time," Christopher said, correctly reading Russell's pensive expression.

"You don't mind, do you?"

His brother quickly waved off his concerns and

returned to pounding him affectionately on the back. "No, no. Of course not."

"Thanks. I'll shower and change into something for the press conference."

"Something casual," Christopher coached, and headed for the door. "Do you want me to send Coleman up? He's great at picking out clothes."

"No. I think I can handle it on my own." Russell's smile tightened again. Did wealthy people need someone else to do everything for them?

"Suit yourself," his brother said over his shoulder. "As a reminder, when you're entertaining a female, staff or otherwise, lock the door."

Russell rolled his eyes and headed to take his shower. The thought of the pending test results and press release kept his anxiety high and his nerves shot. What would happen if he weren't Russell Stone? Where would he go? What would he do?

After the shower, he reached for the electric shaver, but stopped before removing the stubbly new growth. He sort of missed the beard and mustache so he decided to keep the five o'clock shadow...for now.

Walking back into the bedroom with only a towel wrapped around his hips, he nearly jumped out of his skin when he found his bed occupied by the very curvy and very nude Denitra.

"Hello, Russell," she purred, rocking her hips.

He quickly turned his back. "Denitra, what are you doing in here?" He listened as she shifted on the bed.

"I came to see you, silly. So why don't you come over here and say 'hi'?"

Damn. He didn't need to keep the door locked to keep women in, but to keep them out.

"Uh, I'm, uh…" He glanced at his hand and, for the first time, wondered about his absent wedding band.

"Uh—"

"Don't worry," she said, suddenly behind him and pressing her breasts against his back. "There's no need to be shy." She kissed his shoulders. "I can be discreet."

Russell jumped forward and out of her reach. "That's not necessary. I'm a married man and you're—you're with Shaw, remember?"

"Oh, poo on Shaw. You think I don't know he's jumpin' ship the moment his half of the reward money clears the bank?" Denitra came up behind him again and slid her hand across his back. "I'm looking to upgrade. A man of your power and wealth…"

He faced her with narrowed eyes. "My wealth?"

She shrugged lightly. "C'mon, Russell. I didn't mean it like that…"

"I think you should leave," Russell said, and clasped her by the elbow, grabbed her robe from the bed and directed her toward the door.

"Wait," Denitra whined. "I didn't mean to upset you. I just—"

"Wanted to upgrade," he finished for her, and opened the door. On the other side, an attractive woman in a too-tight, black-and-white maid uniform with her breasts clearly ready to spill out of it, stood poised to knock.

"You've got to be kidding me," Russell said to no one in particular.

After Madeline nearly paced a hole in her office carpet, she stood by her icy cold window and watched the holiday's first snow flurries scatter across the Manhattan landscape. News of Christopher and Russell's one-o'clock press conference overloaded the receptionist's switchboard. Media outlets wanted to know whether she would be in attendance. If not, why?

"Why?" she whispered perhaps for the millionth time since Russell's return. It was a big question. A question that encompassed so much.

Of course, all the pain, hurt and confusion would go away if the tests results proved this man wasn't her husband. Was it too much to hope for?

She closed her eyes through a deep sigh and for a fleeting moment the heady taste of Russell's kiss the other night surfaced from her memory. It *was* different. It was tender, sweet—just plain old *better.*

The phone rang and jolted her out of her reverie. It was her direct line and with it being ten minutes til one, she guessed the caller before reading it on the phone's digital caller ID.

She drew a deep breath and picked up the line. "Madeline Stone." Her heartbeat thumped in her ears.

Christopher's somber voice came onto the line. "Hello, Maddie. The test results are in."

She nodded and drew another deep breath.

"It's him," Christopher croaked on a sob. "It's really him."

Madeline didn't remember hanging up.

Chapter 11

New Yorkers woke to a blanket of snow on the first day of December. An undeniable magic weaved its way into the air and elevated the Christmas spirit—for everyone except Madeline. In the week since Russell's tcst results, she blissfully lived in a quiet world called... denial.

It wasn't easy dodging reporters, insurance agents, Russell *and* her mother, but it was a necessary evil. At least that was what she kept telling herself. However, her nice protective bubble ended the afternoon the children's private school called to let her know Russell had been spotted several times near the school's playground.

"He's going to try and take my babies," she panted, racing out of the building. The midday traffic crawl transformed her into a raving lunatic behind the wheel of her expensive, imported sedan. "Get the hell out of the way," she screamed to one of what looked like a flood of yellow taxicabs.

An hour later, she finally reached her destination and bolted out of her car like a bat out of hell.

"Madeline." She heard a familiar voice calling to her.

She twirled so fast she lost her footing on a patch of black ice. Arms and legs flailed during her brief stint in the air and when she landed something cracked.

Russell magically appeared at her side. "Oh, God, Madeline. Are you all right?"

"Something's broke," she said, warding off his assistance, but too fearful to move.

"Are you sure? Let me see if I can help you," Russell said. As he bent down to her side concern swathed his expression.

Madeline didn't move. She couldn't. Seeing him cloaked in black with a thin, groomed goatee caused her stomach to twist in large knots and the casual touch of his hand against her arm sent enough electricity through her to make her forget about sitting in a pile of snow.

What would he do if she leaned forward and kissed him right now?

"Madeline," he said, snapping her out of her ridiculous haze. "Give me your arm and I'll help you up."

She opened her mouth to protest, but he placed a silencing finger against her lips.

"Your other option is to just sit here in a pile of snow like a crybaby until someone feels sorry enough for you to call an ambulance," he ended with a wink. "Now, give me your hand."

Madeline bit her lower lip, instead of chomping down on Russell's finger, and grudgingly placed her hand in his. What she didn't expect was to be lifted effortlessly and hugged up against his broad chest.

Stay calm, she told herself.

Her eyes traveled upward and locked with his dark, liquid gaze. A sensation of drowning flooded her senses and it wasn't until her lungs begged for air that she forced herself to break the trance and suck in a much needed breath.

"Are you all right?" he asked, voice quivering.

She remembered her foot, but realized he was supporting most of her weight. "Let me go," she ordered.

"Are you sure?"

"I said let go." Either the mistake was shoving when he was releasing her or him releasing her when she was shoving because the next thing she knew her butt kissed the sidewalk again. The crack was now a snap and she hollered out in pain.

"Oh, Madeline. I'm so sorry." He scooped down and swept her up into his arms. A gallant move that surprised and impressed her. "Maybe you do need a doctor," he said as he carried her across the parking lot.

Somehow being cocooned in Russell's arm zapped what few brain cells she had left and it wasn't until she was nestled in the backseat of a sleek limousine that she thought to question him. "Wait, where are you taking me?"

Russell, who had climbed into the limo to sit beside her, knocked on the thin Plexiglas. "To the nearest hospital," he shouted.

Madeline laughed. "You know that button by your head works as a intercom."

Russell glanced at the white button and his

face darkened in embarrassment. "That explains the weird looks the driver's been giving me the past few days."

The limo pulled away from the curve.

Shaking her head, she tried to reposition herself so that their legs wouldn't touch, but the shooting pain in her foot forced her to abandon the notion.

"Do you find me repulsive?" Russell studied her for a reaction.

"What were you doing at my children's school?" she asked, changing the subject.

"*Our* children," he corrected. "Why haven't you returned any of my phone calls?"

"I've been busy." She sulked and turned her attention to the passing scenery.

"I just want to see the kids. I wasn't going to do anything like snatch them off the playground."

She folded her arms and continued to sulk.

"That is what you thought, isn't it? That's the reason you raced over there," he said.

Slowly, she turned her head and faced him. "Just like you knew I would."

The bastard actually smiled and for some crazy reason she joined him. They rode in silence for a few minutes before she said, "I was going to call you."

"Really? When?"

A deep breath and then, "As soon as I figured out what to tell Ariel and Russ. Even though they're already asking questions, thanks to their nosey teachers and classmates."

"It's been a week," he said.

"So what's a few more?" He narrowed his dark gaze and caused an army of goose bumps to pimple her skin. "I was joking," she said.

"Sure you were." He leaned over and looked at her feet. He examined how the right one was positioned. "That doesn't look good."

She followed his gaze with a ripple of fear. And sure enough an hour and a half later, the emergency-room intern at Mount Siani Hospital confirmed she had broken her foot.

"You'll need to stay off of it and if it's at all possible keep it elevated," the young intern advised. "Are you her husband?"

The question threw Russell off guard for a moment, but he finally recovered. "Yes," he said firmly.

"Good. Then you'll make sure that she stays off this foot?"

"Yes, sir." Russell saluted and then frowned.

Madeline returned to sulking. "I don't need a babysitter and I have a company to run."

"Either take care of the leg or the leg will take care of you," the intern quipped, and survived one of Madeline's searing stares. "If the foot doesn't heal properly, I guess we could always break it and try again. Of course, you'll run the risk of having ankles the size of bowling balls. That's up to you."

"They must hand out smart-ass cards with medical degrees nowadays."

"Actually," the intern said, and smiled as he headed toward the door, "they do. I'll get someone in here to put on a cast for you."

Russell crossed his arms. "Do you generally pick fights with everyone you come in contact with?"

"It's part of my winning personality," Madeline said.

He laughed, a deep rumble that vibrated the space between them. Funny, how she never noticed that before.

"You know, I think it would be fun looking after you."

"Again. I don't need you looking after me."

"Ah, that's right. You probably have a full staff waiting on you hand and foot already."

"I do not…entirely. And that is beside the point."

"I'm moving in anyway," he announced, crossing his arm.

"Over my dead body."

"It's my house, too."

"I knew you'd pull something like this!" She went to swing her legs off the table, but the pain warned her that it wasn't a smart move, forcing her to wage war propped up on the gurney.

"You figured me out. I'm an evil person for moving back into my house and getting to know my kids," he said. He held up his wrist. "Slap the handcuffs on me. You caught me."

"You're so not funny," Madeline said.

"And you're not being fair."

"Fair? You want to talk to me about being fair?"

Russell cut her off with a silencing finger to her lips. "This relationship will go a lot further if you'd learn to let the past go."

She slapped his hand away and sputtered.

"I can't argue with you," he continued. "I don't remember what our marriage was like. I can't even imagine any kind of marriage based solely on money."

The statement was like a pinprick to her balloon of anger.

"I do know, if it requires me to apologize to you

everyday until we can sort this whole mess out, then fine. I'm sorry."

How in the hell could she continue to be mad at someone who refused to argue with her? It really did take the fun out of things, she thought.

"Would it help if I *asked* to move in?"

Feeling another sulking fit coming on, Madeline dropped her gaze with a halfhearted shrug. Even as she did it, she was mystified by her behavior.

Russell reached out and tipped her chin up so that their eyes could meet. "Madeline, can I move in with you and the children? I want to get to know them…and I want to get to know you," he said softly.

Madeline's hands balled into tight fists as if clinging onto a lifeline. It didn't help.

"May I?" he asked.

"Yes," she finally whispered. "Yes, you may."

Chapter 12

Russ and Ariel eyed their father from behind their mother's legs and crutches. Seeing their trepidation had Madeline kicking herself for not doing a better job preparing them for this moment. Either way, it was too late to go back to a world of denial.

Russell kneeled so he could be eye level with the children and he smiled in a way that melted the hard edges around Madeline's jaded heart.

"Hello, it's so nice to finally meet you two," he said patiently, gazing at them as if he'd never seen anything so beautiful.

"Are you really our father?" Russ asked cautiously, and then ducked back behind his mother.

Russell's smile slid wider and his eyes even twinkled. "Yes. I'm your father."

"Bobby Olson said that you have annameseah," Russ said, butchering the word.

Ariel tugged Madeline's leg. "Momma, what's annameseah?"

"It's amnesia, baby," Madeline corrected. "And it's when someone can't remember the past." Awkwardly, she reached down and tugged on a fat pigtail.

Her daughter frowned pensively. "Like this morning when you couldn't remember where you'd place your car keys?"

Russell chuckled and drew the children's attention back to him. "It's a little more serious than that," he explained. "It's when you can't remember anything. I don't remember being a little boy or who my parents were. Where I grew up," he said, and glanced up. "Or how I met your mother."

Ariel's eyes widened. "How can you forget something like that?"

"I don't know." Russell shrugged. "Dr. Rountree says I must have hurt my heard in the airplane crash."

Curious, Ariel stepped forward first, squinting at her father as if doing so she'd be able to discern the truth. "Does your head hurt?"

"Sometimes."

The confession surprised Madeline. It hadn't occurred to her inquire about any injuries or pain Russell might be having. That was mainly because the old Russell would have whined endlessly about something as small as a paper cut.

"Is that why you've been gone so long? You forgot where you lived?" Russ asked, stepping forward.

"Something like that," Russell said.

Ariel took another step as if proving she was the bravest. "One time, cousin Lysandra got lost at a store and I couldn't find her anywhere. I got really scared. Did you get scared?"

Actually, Ariel had a habit of wandering away in big places. Everyone in the family has experienced an Ariel stress attack at least once.

"It is a little scary," Russell admitted. "But I'm happy to finally find my way home again... to meet you two...to see how beautiful and handsome you are."

A few more steps and Russ took the lead to stand directly in front of his father. "I got a new Tyrannosaurus for my birthday. Do you like dinosaurs?"

Russell thought the question over while maintaining his smile. "I think I do."

Russ's face lit up as he grabbed his father's hand and pulled him forward. "Wait until you see my collection. It's really cool, huh, Mom?"

"Yes, baby. It's really cool," Madeline said.

"Wait. I want him to see my baby-doll collection," Ariel insisted, taking Russell's other hand and pulling him in the opposite direction.

Madeline's heart squeezed painfully in her chest and she forced herself to look away. For the past six years she'd had her babies all to herself. She had owned their laughter, joy and love. And in the snap of a finger, she had to share them. It hurt that they accepted him so easily.

Her hands tightened on the crutches and she turned to wobble away, then Russell's gentle voice floated out to her. "Do you need any help?"

She faced him again and was surprised to see him standing so close. The sudden weakness in her knees made her grateful the crutches supported most of her weight. "No. I'll be all right. I'm sure Consuela won't mind cooking dinner tonight."

"You have a cook?" he asked, disappointed, and then added, "Of course you do."

"And what is *that* supposed to mean?" she asked, defensive.

"Nothing." He shrugged. "I guess I'm just not used to having so many people working for or waiting on me all the time."

Her brows stretched delicately to the center of her forehead. "What, are you a comedian now? You grew up with servants," she said.

He blinked in the face of her anger.

"Or are you trying to say that I'm a lousy mother because I don't have time to cook home-made meals?"

"Mommy doesn't know how to cook," Ariel piped up with a bright smile.

"That's not true," Russ defended his mother. "She can make Jell-O and pudding, bake cookies and—"

"Thank you, Russ," Madeline said, and flashed her son an embarrassed smile. "All right. So I can't cook. That doesn't make me a bad mother."

"How could I ever look at these two," he said gently caressing each of the children's faces, "and think you were anything but an excellent mother?"

Madeline's gaze narrowed. It was going to take

a long time to get use to Russell's free-flowing compliments.

"Maybe I do need to go lay down," she decided.

"Here, let me help. If you just tell me where your bedroom is."

He reached for her, but she avoided him. Not out of pride, Madeline evaded him to avert the havoc that he caused on her senses by simply touching her. Plus, the last place she wanted him was in her bedroom.

"That's all right. I'll manage."

Russell tossed up his hands and stepped back. "As you wish."

The children watched the exchange with curious looks and Madeline attempted to smooth things over with a synthetic smile. "Baths at eight o'clock and then I'll tuck you in."

"That's okay. Why don't you just rest? I'll tuck them in," Russell injected, eagerly.

Madeline stiffened. "I always tuck them in at night."

"That's all right, Mommy," Ariel said. "I want Daddy to tuck me in tonight."

Daddy? Weren't they accepting the man a little too fast? They had just him, for crying out loud.

"I really don't mind," Russell added.

Of course he doesn't. Madeline squirmed, stifling the urge to throw a hissy fit. "Fine," she spat. "You tuck them in." She turned, swinging her crutches to perform a sorry wobbly walk/run combination that undoubtedly gave Russell and the kids a good chuckle.

When she finally reached her bedroom, after a long hike up a deep staircase, she made sure to slam the door with what little strength she had left.

Five minutes later, she sobbed into her pillow. She didn't want to share her children. She didn't want Russell in her house. And she certainly didn't want to be attracted to him. If it wasn't for bad luck she would have no luck at all, she mused.

Two hours later, she was all cried out and suffering an incredible migraine. Somehow, someway she needed to pull herself together.

"Just bide your time. Don't rock the boat until after the House of Madeline launches," she told herself. She nodded through her new mantra. "After that, divorce court, here I come."

A soft knock drew her out of her reverie and she sat up in bed. "Who is it?" she asked timidly.

"It's me. Russell."

"Damn." She mopped her tears with her hands

and pinched her cheeks to pump life back into her face. "What is it?"

When the door cracked open, she thought she was prepared to see her husband; but once again, the moment he appeared his larger-than-life presence seemed to shrink the spacious bedroom. Not to mention, he was in the very room she'd hoped to keep him out of.

"The kids have eaten and are taking their baths. I figure we both could tuck them in tonight."

Another peace offering. The man was so unpredictable.

"That's okay. They seem to really want you to do it."

"Look," he said, closing the door and moving deeper into the room. "I'm not trying to step on any toes here and I definitely don't want to disrupt any routine you have going."

"Well, you're just an all around good guy, huh?" she said with biting sarcasm.

To this, he simply laughed.

"What's so funny?"

"Do you really have to ask?"

She didn't so she was left to work her jaw in silence.

"What do we have to do to get past this?" he asked, crossing his arms.

Madeline said nothing.

"Do you want a divorce? Is that what all this is leading to?"

Her eyes snapped to his and her heart suddenly lodged in the center of her throat, suffocating her. Now that the subject hung heavy in the air, an unexpected fear tangled with her conflicting emotions.

Russell cocked his head while his eyes continued studying her. "You're thinking," he said, sliding his hands into his pants pockets and inching toward the bed. "You're thinking about the money."

Madeline pressed back against the pillows, her breath thinning as he approached.

"Is it truly all that's between us?"

She wanted to say "yes," but she couldn't get the word out of her mouth.

"Because I don't think so. It's not what I feel when I look at you." He stopped at the edge of the bed with such passion in his eyes she didn't know how it was possible her clothes hadn't melted off her body.

"What are you doing?" she squeaked.

"Nothing. I just want to talk with you." He sat on the edge of the bed, close to her broken foot.

She planted her arms at her side and wiggled farther away from him.

As he watched, disappointment rippled across his features. Silently, he reached for one of the bed's throw pillows and gently lifted her leg and placed the pillow under her foot.

A slow heat stretched all the way up her leg and then simmered in the center of her body.

"Can I ask you a question?"

"You just did," she whispered.

He smiled and she tried to ignore the ache pulsing between her legs, but the harder she tried, the more intense it became. What if she slightly spread her legs? Would his hand roam higher?

In a flash, Russell's smile disappeared. "Were you upset when my plane crashed? Did you cry for me?"

Chapter 13

"Please tell me you lied to him this time,"
Lysandra begged Madeline the next morning.
"Just don't tell me you confessed about the wid-
ow party you threw."

"Of course I didn't tell him about the party,"
Madeline snapped while digging a wire coat
hanger down the side of her leg cast. She'd only
had the thing on one day and already she had an
itch that was positively driving her crazy.

"So what did you say?" Lysandra asked,
setting the House of Madeline fall-collection

sketches down on the bed. "Or do I really want to know?"

Madeline dropped the hanger and tossed her hands up in the air. "I lied. Okay?" She rocked back against the pillows, but ended up slamming her head against the headboard. "Ow. Damn it," she hissed.

Lysandra's shoulders deflated with relief. "Well, thank God. I thought you'd totally lost your mind this past week."

"Always my voice of reason." Madeline reached for the crutches beside the bed and allowed her cousin to assist her out of the bed. One of the good things about having to work out of her bedroom on a Saturday was the luxury of wearing silk pajamas all day.

"Joke if you want to, but I have a vested interest in House of Madeline, too."

It was true. Lysandra had left a hard-earned career with Chanel and was taking a big gamble with the House of Madeline. If they failed, she would be starting from ground zero. Either that or enlist Cecelia to help find her a millionaire husband.

"Everything is under control," Madeline said.

"What did you say about the divorce?"

Drawing a deep breath, she hobbled to the

bedroom's bay window and then blinked in surprise to see Russell and Russ in the middle of the
lush green estate tossing her son's beloved
football. She couldn't ever remember seeing her
little boy so happy. The realization of how much
he needed his father in his life was like a sucker
punch to her gut. It caused another wave of inse-
curity to wash over her.

For six years she thought she'd been doing a
good job being both mother and father. Now seeing
her children with their real father, their easy accep-
tance of him, made her question everything.

"Maddie?" Lysandra placed a hand on her
shoulder. "Why are you crying?"

Madeline placed her hand against her cheek,
stunned to find it wet with tears.

Lysandra glanced out of the window in time to
see Ariel charge out onto the grass and tackle her
brother onto the ground. Both women laughed as
Russ pretended to be wounded while Ariel grabbed
the football and raced for a make-believe touch-
down.

"She hates sports," Madeline whispered.

Lysandra wrapped an arm around her cousin's
shoulders. "Don't make this about you," she said.
"You are a wonderful mother."

Madeline clung to the affirmation as though it was a life raft in a sea during a perfect storm.

"I still can't believe it's him," Lysandra said. Her gaze centered on Russell. "Hell, I didn't think he knew anything about sports."

"I'm sure Russ nagged him to play."

"Still, he has a pretty good arm," she noted.

Lysandra turned away from the window. "I better order up some coffee so we can get started going over some of these sketches."

Madeline nodded and continued to gaze out of the window. Her family was quite beautiful and their ringing laughter succeeded in carving a smile on her face.

Russell glanced up and shielded his eyes from the sun and met her stare with his own smile. Despite the distance, a wild fluttering erupted in the pit of her stomach and breathing became difficult again.

Russ and Ariel followed their father's gaze to see what had drawn his attention. When they spotted their mother, they waved frantically. Blinking back her tears, Madeline signaled back.

She turned away from the window and then stopped beneath Lysandra's tight scrutiny. "What?"

Her cousin shrugged her shoulders, but a smile bloomed across her face.

"What?" Madeline pressed.

Lysandra crossed her arms in a superior stance. "You like him."

Madeline's face burned with embarrassment. "Oh, don't be ridiculous. You know I can't stand the man."

"I know you *used* to couldn't stand him. The old Russell Stone wouldn't have swept you up off the sidewalk and carried you to the hospital emergency room. He also wouldn't have tucked the children into bed or have played touch football in the front yard like some overgrown kid. But the new Russell…he's getting under your skin," Lysandra said.

Madeline swallowed and hobbled away from the window. "You're imagining things."

"Uh-huh." Lysandra smiled and shook her head.

Madeline clamped her mouth shut and returned to the bed and threw herself into work. Well, she tried anyway. It was hard to concentrate with Russell and the children laughing and playing beneath her window.

How come she never learned to throw a football? It was clearly Russ's favorite sport and now Ariel seemed fond of it, as well. The questions chased one another inside of her head until long after the laughter disappeared and there was a knock on her door.

"Come in," she said without looking up.

"Afternoon, ladies," Russell said.

Madeline and Lysandra both looked up from the bed's array of paperwork to see Russell pushing in a silver wheelchair carrying both Russ and Ariel.

"Look what Daddy got you, Mommy," Ariel squealed, jumping out of the chair.

Russell beamed with his chest puffed out. "I figure this will make it a lot easier for you to get around *and* to keep your leg elevated."

"How very thoughtful," Lysandra said, glancing over at her cousin. "Isn't that thoughtful, Maddie?"

Madeline wished someone thought to bring her a baseball bat, as well, so she could knock a few of Lysandra's teeth out. "Yes, it's very thoughtful," she seethed. "But unnecessary or not very practical given the number of stairs in this place."

Her comment shaved a few inches off Russell's handsome face.

"You can always use the service elevators," Russ said, popping out of the chair and rushing over to tug on her arm. "Come on and take a ride. Lunch is ready downstairs."

Madeline still hesitated.

"Do you really hate the wheelchair, or is it the fact that it's from me?" Russell asked bluntly.

Once again, Madeline found herself shifting uncomfortably beneath a room full of expectant gazes. "I didn't say I hated the wheelchair." She struggled to stand, but not for long. Russell quickly appeared at her side and helped her up.

Her body responded to every touch of his hand and there was so much heat generating between them, she feared at any moment she'd pass out from it's intensity. Finally she was secured in the wheelchair with her broken leg propped up.

"Can I ride in your lap, Mommy?" Ariel asked.

"Sure, baby. Climb on up," Madeline said.

"Daddy, can I help push?" Russ asked.

"Can you?" Russell echoed. "I insist on it."

Lysandra watched the whole family exchange with a wide knowing smile. "You know, I better get going," she said, reaching for her purse. "I promised a friend we could get some Christmas shopping in today."

Madeline knew her cousin well enough to know when she was lying. "What friend?"

"Believe it or not I do have friends, Maddie," Lysandra said.

"Can it wait until after lunch?" Russell asked. "We have plenty. It will also give me the chance to get to know you...again."

Lysandra laughed, but remained firm on leaving. "Another time," she promised.

Russ and Russell wheeled Madeline and Ariel down to the dining room where bowls of hot, hearty chili awaited them to knock off the winter chill.

Madeline discovered there was no reason to wish she'd been playing with Russell and the children in the yard, because Russ and Ariel were more than happy to give her a blow-by-blow account of their game.

"I can almost throw the ball as far as Russ," Ariel bragged.

"Can not." Russ frowned and gave a playful tug on her braided pigtail.

"Can, too. Can't I, Daddy?"

"Sure can, pumpkin."

Pumpkin? He'd already assigned them pet names? She slapped her head into the palm of her hand and groaned. This whole thing continued to go way too fast for her.

"Madeline," Russell said. "Are you feeling all right?"

"Peachy," she lied, and avoided his gaze.

After lunch, Madeline made her excuses to return to her work, but Ariel insisted she stay with them and play board games.

Russ groaned, wanting to return to his beloved football game.

"You promised," Ariel reminded him, jutting up her chin.

"You did promise," Russell said. "A man should never break his promise."

The bark of laughter was out of Madeline's throat before she had a chance to stop herself.

"You disagree?" Russell asked with raised eyebrows.

"No," she said. "Of course not." It was just that she'd never known him to keep any of his promises, but that was a conversation for another time.

Russell waited until their gazes met and when they did there was no mistaking his disappointment in her constant needling about his past.

"Sorry," she whispered, feeling like a chastised child.

The board games had mainly been purchased for the kids and their friends. Madeline was ashamed she'd never sat at a table and played the games with Russ and Ariel. As it turned out, Ariel was a world champion at Candyland, Chutes and Ladders and even Sorry!

"She has to be cheating," Russ complained.

"Am not! You're just a sorry loser," Ariel charged back.

"All right, you two," Madeline refereed. "No one likes a 'sore' loser, Russ."

"Yes, ma'am," he said contrite, but then stuck his tongue out at his sister.

"Mommy, are you going to help us put up Christmas decorations?"

"What?" Madeline's gaze cut over to her husband. It was his turn to look apologetic.

"Uh, yeah. I told the staff not to bother with the decorations this morning. I figured we would put them up ourselves," Russell said.

"Daddy says tomorrow we can even go pick out our own tree," Russ added.

"But we order our tree every year from Mountain Star Tree Farm." Madeline noted how quickly the children's faces fell after that announcement and she resented being cast as the party pooper.

Russell cleared his throat. "I just thought it would be a lot more fun if we all went and selected a tree as a family."

Madeline crossed her arms and glared. "You did, did you? And what do you know about picking out Christmas trees?" She shouldn't have snapped, she realized. The children's gazes darted between their parents while Russell's jaw tightened.

"I just don't see the point of having everything done for us. It wouldn't hurt to get our hands dirty every once in a while," he said.

"Spoken like man born with a silver spoon in his mouth."

Fire lit behind his narrowed gaze but he managed to keep his voice cool and under control. "The sarcasm is getting old." He put his arms around the kids. "C'mon. Let's go back outside and play some more touch football. We'll do the decorations after dinner," Russell said.

"Are we still going to shop for our tree tomorrow?" Ariel asked.

Russell's eyes traveled back to Madeline. "That's up to your mother."

Ariel and Russell rushed to Madeline's side with wide-eyed eagerness. "Can we, Momma? Can we?"

One look into their faces and there was no way she was going to deny them anything and perhaps leaving the decision to her was Russell's way of letting her come out looking like a hero instead of the bad mother.

"Of course we can," she said.

Russ and Ariel erupted into cheers and even took turns planting kisses on her upturned cheek before running out of the room.

"I'll be out in a minute," he announced to their retreating backs and then lingered in the dining room.

A few seconds ticked in silence, before Madeline blurted out, "I'm sorry." She swallowed the painful lump in her throat and continued, "It's really hard for me to get used to this whole…thing. *They* don't seem to have a problem with it, but…"

"I understand," he said. "It's hard for me, too."

Her anger deflated. In that moment, she realized she needed to figure out some way to let the past stay in the past; if not for her, at least for the children's sake.

"Truce?" he asked.

Tears stung Madeline's eyes. She blinked them away and arrived at a decision she prayed she wouldn't regret. "Truce."

Chapter 14

Russell fell deeper in love every time his daughter made her Woody Woodpecker laugh. After a day of frolicking in the winter cold, whooping everyone in board games and now leading the family in off-tuned Christmas carols, Ariel's laughter infected everyone.

There were a few moments, fleeting ones, when Russell experienced a strong sense of déjà vu. Stringing up lights, hanging up wreaths and pinning up the occasional mistletoe. During those moments, a warm glow would spread throughout his body and deliver an unexplainable peace. Then in the next second, it was gone.

"Can I help put this one up over there, Daddy?" Ariel asked, referring to a shimmering multicolored garland.

"You sure can," he said, and picked her up. She released another hearty laugh as he set her on his broad shoulders. All the while, he was more than aware of how Madeline's gaze followed him.

To his great relief their "truce" remained in effect and as the evening progressed, he watched her loosen up, laugh and even sing—though she was the main person off-key. She was adorable really, wheeling around the room, taping holiday cards along the fireplace and even participating in some silent competition with Russ on who could eat the most mini candy canes.

"Mommy, can we do this every Christmas?" Russ asked, setting out nutcrackers that were as tall as he was around the room.

"Of course we can," she said, pinching his cheeks.

Russell smiled and took great pride for having such a beautiful family. How could he have ever taken such a thing for granted? Again this morning he had to fight off two more advances from women who worked in his home under threat of termination. Who had ever heard of sexual harassment from one's employees? he wondered.

At this point, he'd drawn the conclusion that in his previous life he had either a serious sex or mental problem. No wonder Madeline hated him.

The one question that played over in his head was also the one he feared to give voice to. Did Madeline ever step outside of the marriage? Not just in the six years since he'd been missing, but while they were together. Who did she turn to when she couldn't turn to him?

"What do you say we light the fireplace and roast some marshmallows and make some s'mores?"

"Yea!" the children cheered.

Madeline laughed, shaking her head. "What do you know about making s'mores?"

"Aw." He waved off the question. "Used to make them all the time at camp." He stopped when he realized what he'd said and then looked at his wife.

"You used to go to camp?"

"I-I must have." He stopped and tried to remember, but all he got was the beginnings of a headache.

"Don't worry," she said. "It'll all come back to you in time."

He fluttered a half smile and wished for the first time that he could pick and choose which memories to recall.

The family strolled off down the long hallway to go raid the kitchen cabinets.

"Daddy, are we going to decorate the whole house?" Ariel asked from her high perch on his shoulders.

Russell glanced around thinking it would take the whole Christmas season to decorate the entire house. "We could definitely give it a try."

Madeline and Russ laughed from behind them. He turned to see his son had climbed into his mother's lap and was manning the electric-power controls in time to jump out of the way before being run over.

"Hey," he shouted, feigning outrage. "You two better slow down before I give you a ticket."

"I wanna ride," Ariel complained.

Russell pretended that being dumped by his daughter didn't hurt a bit, but his disappointment was short lived when Russ hopped out of his mother's lap to jump on his back.

When they reached the main kitchen, Russell

gave a low impressive whistle at the sheer size of the place. "Is this a kitchen or a mess hall?"

"Very funny," Madeline commented, and then watched as the children tore into the stainless steel cabinets.

"I found the marshmallows!" Ariel declared.

"I got the graham crackers!" Russ announced proudly.

"And I have the chocolate," Madeline said, pulling out a bottle of Hershey's Chocolate Syrup. Her shoulders shrank after her prideful boast beneath everyone's questioning stare. "What? Everything tastes better with chocolate."

"Really?" Russell's brows shot up as he gave her a flirtatious wink and extracted the bottle from her hands, their fingertips brushing. "I'm going to have to try and remember that."

"But, Daddy, you can't remember anything because of your annameseah."

Russell and Madeline laughed and turned to make their trek back to the living room. However, the moment Madeline and Russell crossed the wide archway, Ariel screamed and bounced excitedly on her toes.

"Uh-oh. You're under the mistletoe," she chanted.

Russ just shook his head.

"You know what that means, Daddy. You gotta kiss Mommy."

Russell looked down at his wife. Madeline looked as if she would rather superglue her lips to fly paper. But ignoring her hands-off body language, Russell shrugged. "Rules are rules."

He leaned over, fascinated by how wide her eyes rounded. Stopping just inches from her lips, he whispered, "You don't mind, do you?"

Truth be told, he was kissing her regardless of the answer; but it was still nice to see the slight shake of her head. A small smile curled into place, but disappeared when his lips brushed against hers. There was a sweet, exquisiteness to her lips. The same as it had been at his brother's house when he wanted to lose himself in the very taste of her.

Ariel erupted into giggle, and when Russell turned to look at the kids, Russ just shook his head as if he didn't get the whole kissing thing.

Russell laughed, but when he turned back to see how Madeline reacted to the kiss, she'd already hit the forward button on her chair to escape the mistletoe or him or maybe both.

Before long, a nice fire crackled in the fireplace and skewered marshmallows were being roasted, sandwiched and dipped in chocolate syrup. Everyone was propped on floor pillows—Madeline included—giggling, laughing and generally enjoying the winter night until tiny mouths yawned and little eyelids drooped with sleep.

Smiling, Russell watched his children's angelic faces as they drifted off to dreamland.

"They're precious, aren't they?" Madeline whispered.

He nodded. "I've missed so much," he replied. "Lost so much." His fingers drifted down the side of Ariel's chubby cheeks.

Empathy tugged at Madeline's soul and tears welled behind her eyes. The constant conflicting emotions grew exhausting and she wondered just how long she would be able to take it.

"You really have done a wonderful job with them," Russell said, voice cracking. "They're smart, love to laugh and play. They're just so full of life."

"They also seem to like you a lot," she said, attempting to salve his pain.

His short smile looked more like a tic. "You're not too happy about that."

She didn't respond. She couldn't.

"Maybe we should get these two in bed." He stood and helped Madeline into her chair. Next, he gently scooped Ariel off the floor and placed her in her mother's arms.

Madeline hit the forward button on her chair while, Russell extracted Russ from the floor and then followed her to the service elevator. Upstairs they split up to take the kids to their separate bedrooms.

Russ's head had barely touched the pillow when his eyes fluttered open and a large yawn stretched his mouth. "Daddy?"

In the glow of the nightlight, Russell gazed down at his son. "Yeah, sport?"

"You're going to be here in the morning, right? You're not going to forget about us again, are you?"

Tears rolled from Russell's eyes before he had a chance to stop them, but he still managed a reassuring smile. "I'll be here and I'm never going to forget you again."

Russ smiled and curled into his pillow. "'Night, dad."

"Good night, son." Russell leaned forward and brushed a kiss against the boy's temple. In the next second, his son was fast asleep and he was content to just watch him throughout the night.

After a while, Madeline filled the doorway. The wheelchair gone, but the crutches returned.

"Needed to stretch my legs," she whispered, and then nodded at Russ. "Is everything okay?"

"Yeah." Russell fluttered one last smile down at his son and then finally stood and left the room. In the hallway, a deafening silence enveloped them.

It wasn't that Russell didn't have anything to say. Truth of the matter was that he had too much to say, too many questions, like: was there any hope in saving their marriage? Could she ever truly forgive and forget?

Of course, he had an advantage on the forgetting part.

However, he was sure talking about any of the issues between them would destroy their fragile truce. Talking was bad. Now, kissing, that was another story all together. His gaze lowered to her full lips and the temperature in the house jumped a good fifty degrees.

"Well," she said, "I better go to bed, too."

An instant picture of Madeline draped across satin sheets filled his head and he didn't know whether the image was a memory or a fantasy. "Then, I guess I should say good-night," he said as a statement, but it sounded more like a question to his ears.

Madeline nodded but she made no move toward

the master bedroom at the end of the hallway. She looked as though she wanted to tell him something.

"Do you need any help?" he asked lamely.

She shook her head and drew a deep breath. "I want to thank you," she finally blurted out. "For today. The kids really had a nice time."

He nodded while he tried to commit every detail of her face to memory.

"I had a nice time," she added.

A small ripple of laughter passed his lips. "That must have been real hard for you to say."

She smiled. "Painful." Finally, she turned and headed toward her bedroom.

He followed, not sure why, but glad that she didn't question him. At the doorway, she faced him, undoubtedly to say good-night. However, he robbed her of the chance when he surprised her with a kiss. It was probably the wrong thing to do, but he couldn't help himself. The taste of her had lingered on his lips since the mistletoe incident and he knew if he'd asked to kiss her again, the answer would've been no.

The crutches fell from her arms and hit the floor with a loud bang while Madeline leaned into him with an audible sigh. The important thing was that she kissed him back with a hunger that drained what little logic he had left in his head.

Whatever her reasons, he wasn't going to question them. Instead, he scooped his wife into his arms and carried her over to the bed—their lips never parting once. The mattress dipped beneath their combined weight. Russell remained careful with her injured leg as he hovered above her. Like before, he couldn't get enough.

"Oh, God," she breathed the moment she came up for air.

When Russell's lips skimmed the column of her neck, she quivered in his arms.

"We shouldn't be doing this," she panted.

"Why not?" he asked, sucking on her lower earlobe. "We're married." His hands roamed up her soft, quivering body. He carefully pressed his throbbing erection against her inner thigh to let her know just how much he wanted her.

Instead of turning her on, she squirmed away from him. "No," she groaned. "It's not…it's not that simple," she whispered.

"Sure it is." He kissed her again to show her just how easy it was.

As he'd hoped, she returned his kisses and allowed his hands to dip beneath her satin top and her bra. He moaned at the feel of her marbleized nipples.

"I can't. Please…"

Convinced he could still change her mind, Russell shifted his weight and lowered his head to feast on her glorious breasts. The first pleasant surprise was that they were larger than her clothes portrayed; the second surprise was how sweet the light dust of body powder she'd used tasted.

"Oh, God," she moaned, arching her back and filling his mouth even more. "What am I doing?"

Russell's greedy mouth moved to the other breast.

"Please…please."

Russell groaned as he pulled away from his new best friends to look her in the eye. "I won't make love to you, if you don't want me to," he promised. "But I want to make you feel good." His hand drifted to the pants of her pajamas. Their lips met again. "Let me make you feel good." His fingers graze the vee of curls between her legs. "Will you let me do that?"

"Mommy?"

Russell jerked his hand back.

Madeline yanked her pajama top down.

Both heads swiveled toward the door.

Ariel stood in the doorway, hugging a teddy bear and staring wide-eyed at the bed. "Daddy, what are you doing to Mommy?"

Chapter 15

First thing Monday morning at the House of Madeline, Lysandra stared open mouthed at her cousin. "You slept with him?"

"No. I didn't sleep with him," Madeline hissed, crouched over her desk and then straightened in her chair.

"You mean, you would have if Ariel hadn't interrupted?"

"No," she insisted with a little less vigor.

Lysandra crossed her arms as one brow stretched high.

"Don't look at me like that," Madeline threatened. "I was *not* going to sleep with him. I was just…I don't know." She shook her head while Saturday night replayed in her head. *She was still in control of the situation with Russell, wasn't she?*

"Why don't you just admit you're attracted to the guy? I mean, sheesh. He is your husband."

"Because any day now his memory is going to come back and he's going to go right back to being the same old asshole. I'd rather cut my losses and get out now," Madeline said.

"Maybe. Maybe not." Lysandra shrugged. "He definitely doesn't seem like the same guy. It's just as likely what he's been through in the last six years has changed him apparently for the better."

"You believe that?"

"Why not? He returned from the dead, didn't he?"

"I don't know why I talk to you about this stuff." Madeline feigned interest in the budget spreadsheets on her desk.

"It's either me or your mother," her cousin said, and then laughed. "Speaking of which, where is she?"

"I don't know and I'm not looking a gift horse in the mouth," Madeline admitted with a sheepish grin.

"Well, it's the Christmas season and if there's one thing she likes more than hunting for a new husband it's—"

"Shopping," they finished in unison.

Lysandra smiled, took a sip of her coffee and then asked, "Anything happen after you put Ariel back to bed?"

Madeline's eyes remained on the spreadsheets. "I didn't put her back to bed. She slept with me, and Russell returned to the guestroom."

Lysandra choked. "You used your little girl as a human shield? Ha! That's rich."

"I did no such thing," Madeline lied. "Ariel had a bad dream and she usually sleeps with me whenever that happens."

Lysandra shook her head. "If that's your story then…"

"It *is* my story because it's the truth," Madeline snapped, removing her reading glasses.

Lysandra clammed up and took another sip of coffee.

"All right. I had a weak moment. I admit it, but I was not going to sleep with him. I will not.

Whatever truce we have is just for the holidays and the children."

"And the fashion line."

"Right," Madeline agreed. "There are plenty of loveless, sexless marriages in New York. What's one more?"

"Riiiight." Lysandra eyed her cousin, weighing whether Madeline had finally lost her mind.

Madeline wondered the same thing.

"What are you going to do the next time Russell tries to seduce you?"

Madeline worked her jaw, but no answer was forthcoming.

"You do know he's going to try again, don't you?"

She did know and she had no earthly idea what she was going to do about it.

Russell's first day at Stone Cold Records bordered on being an out-of-body experience. Media outlets and curious onlookers surrounded the Manhattan building, making it nearly impossible for the stretch limo to pull up to the front door.

Overwhelmed, Russell stared out of his tinted windows and wondered if he was truly ready. He had no clue on what to do. Was everyone expecting him to say something, or make a speech? He scanned the eager faces, hoping to spot his brother, his life raft, in the crowd.

"Is there a problem, sir?" the driver asked.

Russell swallowed and cleared his throat. "It sure is a lot of people," he said.

"Yes, sir," the driver agreed. "Maybe it would help if you just pictured everyone in their underwear."

"Does that really work?"

"No time like now to find out."

Russell chuckled. "What's your name?"

"Dennis Cameron," the young man said, and smiled as if no one had ever asked him such a simple question before.

"Hi, Dennis." Russell stretched his hand through the divider. "Russell Stone."

"Yes, sir. I know."

"Actually, I'm still trying to get used to the name."

Dennis nodded like such a thing happened all the time.

Russell scanned the crowd again. "Just picture them in their underwear, huh?"

"That's what they say."

Drawing a deep breath, Russell reached for the door. "Well, here goes nothing." He opened the door and a chorus of, "Mr. Stone. Mr. Stone, over here," surrounded him.

Camera's shuttered and a startling amount of lights blinded him.

"Mr. Stone. How are you adjusting to your old life?" a female shouted.

"About as well as to be expected. I'm taking everything one day at a time," he answered.

"What about Lola Crowne? Do you remember what happened to her?"

Russell turned toward the woman who'd voiced the question and wished like hell he had a better answer than the one he was about to give. "I have no recollection of what happened to Ms. Crowne. I wish I did. I'd like nothing more than to be able to offer her family closure."

"Mr. Stone. Mr. Stone," the chorus started up again. This time the questions were hurled simultaneously and at lightening speed.

At last, Christopher parted the crowd and rescued Russell with a magnanimous smile. "That's enough questions for now, guys. You already have my brother here looking like a deer caught in headlights."

Laughter rippled around him while Christopher took hold of Russell's elbow and led him through the front doors. However, another crowd of people awaited him inside the building.

"There's no easy way to do this," Christopher said. He turned to their audience and said, "Everyone, you all remember Russell. Russell this is the staff."

Russell smiled awkwardly with a brief wave. "Hello, everyone."

"Welcome back, Mr. Stone," they shouted in sync, and then exploded with applause.

Russell laughed and tried to relax. It probably had more to do with Christopher being by his side than anything else. He shook hands with a few people and retained only a couple of names. All in all, people tried not to stare, but in the end it seemed they couldn't help themselves.

Christopher did what he could to make things easier, cheesing and telling corny jokes; but nothing really worked. Russell still felt like a fish out of water.

"I figured tonight we could head over to the club, Xotic," he said, walking Russell to his old office. "We have a CD release party. Good time for you get to know one of our artists."

"Tonight?" Russell asked. "Tonight is not a good night."

"You have other plans?" Christopher laughed.

"Well, I was hoping to take Madeline and the kids to see *The Nutcracker.*"

"*The Nutcracker?*"

"Well, yeah." Russell laughed awkwardly. "Ariel said a few of her friends were going and she looked so cute so I—"

"I understand." Christopher pushed open a door and gestured proudly to the room's startling grandeur. "Here's your old office."

It looked more like a penthouse apartment, Russell thought as he entered, his feet sinking into the plush, carpet. One wall of the office was a breathtaking gold-and-bronze water fountain, on the other end a gigantic aquarium with a multitude of colorful fish. There was also a magnificent view of the Manhattan skyline. In between were such toys as a handsome billiard table, minigolf putter, a glass bar, leather sectional sofas, huge stereo system and a...steel pole of some kind.

"You like?" Christopher asked, hope ringing in his voice.

"It's...interesting. Where exactly is the desk?"

"Well, uh, the desk thing wasn't exactly your style. Too structured, you used to say."

"So I played pool and practiced my golf swing all day?"

"Not exactly. Your toys loosened you up, got your creative juices flowing."

"I see," he lied.

Christopher smiled. "Anyway, if there's anything else you can think of that you'll need, your new secretary, Glenda, will be sure to get it for you."

Russell nodded, still looking the place over, this time taking note of the large plasma television hanging from the wall.

"You know, I wish you would really reconsider going to the party tonight. The media following you around would be an extra push for the group."

Swimming through a sea of photographers again held zero appeal for Russell.

"Even a walk through would do. Thirty minutes, an hour tops," Christopher pleaded.

"I don't know," Russell hedged. "I should call Madeline and—"

"Madeline, eh? What, is she wearing the pants in the family now?"

Russell frowned.

"Sure. Sure. I understand. You two, uh, get back together yet? You know, hooked up?"

Brother or not, Russell wasn't comfortable discussing the intimate details of his marriage.

Christopher's head rock back with a hearty laugh. "I didn't think so. Maddie can be a cold bitch when she wants to be."

Russell's smile melted and steam blew out of his ears. "Let's get one thing straight. You don't talk about my wife like that."

Christopher tried to laugh it off, but Russell's expression grew harder by the second.

"All right. All right. My bad. I'm sorry."

Russell nodded, but his expression remained cold.

Christopher glanced at his watch. "We have a lot of meetings lined up for the rest of the day. Why don't you give Madeline a call a little later?"

Ariel looked like a Christmas present in her red velvet dress and her thick hair pulled back and tied with a silver bow. Madeline had never seen her daughter fret so much in front of the mirror, but the child was determined to look good for their first official date out with her father.

Russ, on the other hand, whined and complained for having to wear a suit for the night's show.

"What time is Daddy going to make it home?" Ariel asked for twentieth time in the last five minutes. "The show starts at seven-thirty."

"I know, honey," Madeline glanced at her watch, thinking they were going to be late if they didn't leave in the next five minutes.

"Momma, can I at least wear my Nikes?" Russ asked, fingering his collar.

"Fine. Whatever." At this point, she didn't care if her son wore cowboy boots.

The house phone rang and Madeline's gaze cut toward it, her heart filled with a sudden dread. A second later, Consuela appeared at the doorway.

"Mrs. Stone, your husband is on the line."

"Daddy?" Ariel asked, turning her questioning gaze toward her mother.

Madeline stood with her new silver cane and hobbled to the phone. "Hello."

"Madeline," Russell yelled over hard pounding music. "Thank God I caught you. Look, something has come up. I'm stuck a CD-release party."

"You don't say?" Madeline's shoulders deflated as she shook her head.

"There's no way I can make it to the house in time. Why don't you guys go ahead on over to the show and I'll meet you there?"

Madeline turned her back in a vain attempt to block the conversation. "You *promised* Ariel," she hissed.

"And I'll be there," Russell insisted.

"Yeah, right." She slammed down the phone and muttered a curse under her breath. Looked like Russell Stone had reverted to his old ways of lying and breaking promises.

"Momma?" Ariel tugged on her arm. "Where's Daddy?"

Chapter 16

Russell cursed under his breath and pocketed his new cell phone. He knew before he made the call that Madeline was going to be mad, but there was nothing like hearing her disappointment. Though he didn't remember what their previous life had been like, his wife never missed an opportunity to point out he'd been a lousy husband. Since his return, he'd vowed to be a better husband and father. Heck, he vowed to be a better man all around.

However, this was a challenging feat in the music industry. Beautiful women with barely there clothes and high heels filled Club Xotic. In the hour, Russell turned down several numbers, advances and offers for quickies, blowjobs and hand jobs.

He was definitely not having a good time.

Christopher, on the other hand, seemed to be in his element. Russell watched his brother pocket phone numbers, boldly rub up against a few barely legal women and even disappear a time or two. Each time he returned, he wore a bigger and brighter smile.

"Come on, bro. Relax," Christopher commanded, ordering two drinks from a passing waitress. "This is a party, remember?"

"Yeah, look. I need to get out of here. Madeline is pissed."

"When isn't she pissed?" Christopher laughed.

Russell flashed him a look of warning and his brother quickly apologized.

"I'm sorry. I know you're trying to do the whole 'family guy' thing and that's admirable, but I miss our old hanging days, scoring with the ladies."

"I'm sorry, but I don't think that's really for me," Russell said.

Christopher's boisterous laugh drew more than its share of curious glances. "Please. I know you aren't getting any at home. Madeline kept those legs locked so tight it's a miracle you even have children."

"Are you drunk?"

"Probably. But that doesn't change the facts," Christopher said.

Their drinks arrived and Christopher left a Benjamin Franklin on the waitress's tray with the order to, "keep the change."

"Thank you, Mr. Stone."

Christopher flashed her a cheesy smile and watched her thick booty sashay away from the table. "Now, you can't tell me that you wouldn't like to tap something like that."

Russell followed his gaze and had to admit the woman certainly curved in all the right places.

"Uh-huh. I thought so." Christopher shared a knowing wink with his brother before taking another sip of his drink. "Like I said, relax and pick out something nice and curvy. And don't worry about Madeline. She's not going anywhere."

"What do you mean?"

Christopher shrugged. "I mean just that. As long as the money is good, she's not going anywhere." He drained his glass and his smile slid uneven. "Now that you're back, your ironclad prenuptial agreement is back in effect. I already talked to our family attorney. The moment you walked back into our lives, Madeline's pockets grew considerably lighter. If she walks out, she loses everything, and a woman like Madeline would rather suffer in silence than become penniless."

Russell slumped back in his chair as Stone Cold artist, King Royal, took to the stage. He thought back to when he brought up the subject of divorce to Madeline and how she never answered the question. At the time, he thought her avoiding the question was a reason to give hope for a reconciliation—a chance to start anew.

Now, he didn't know what to think.

The New York City Ballet's performance of *The Nutcracker* was indeed a vision to behold. Ariel sat at the edge of her seat, her eyes following every graceful movement of the dancers. She gasped during the adventures through the Land of Snow and then the Kingdom of Sweets. However, long before "Clara" battled the Mouse King, Russ had leaned against Madeline's arm and dozed off.

"Mommy?" Ariel whispered. "Do you think Daddy's annameseah got him lost again?"

"I don't know, baby." Madeline smiled and gave her daughter's hand a reassuring pat. When Ariel returned her attention back to the stage, Madeline returned to grinding her teeth and cursing out her husband in her head.

Six years ago, she was the only one who suffered through Russell's broken promises. He'd even missed Russ's first birthday party, but her son was too young to remember that. The point was she wasn't looking forward to a lifetime of explaining and mending her children's broken hearts because their father will always have better things to do...and other women to do them with.

"Daddy!" Ariel exclaimed in a loud whisper.

A few audience members shushed the six-year old, but to Madeline's surprise, Russell settled into the seat next to his daughter and delivered a quick kiss against her upturned cheek.

"Sorry I'm late." He glanced over the top of Ariel's head and met Madeline's startled look.

Madeline turned away and tried to act indifferent, but she was doing a lousy job. Seconds later, the house lights came up and Russell groaned.

"Did I miss the whole thing?" He glanced at his watch.

"No, silly," Ariel teased. "It's intermission."

He sighed with visible relief. "Oh, good. Are you enjoying it so far, pumpkin?"

Ariel gave an enthusiastic nod and moved to sit on her father's lap. "Did you forget where we were?"

"No, baby. Uncle Christopher and I had a release party to attend. I left as soon as I could. I'll try to do better next time."

"It's okay. At least you made it. I don't think Mommy thought you would."

Madeline sucked in a small gasp. Betrayed by her baby.

"Is that right?" Russell questioned. "Well, it looks like she was wrong, doesn't it?"

Ariel dutifully bobbed her head.

"And don't you look beautiful tonight." He complimented his daughter. "Stand up and twirl around so I can take a good look."

Giggling as she leapt up from her father's lap, Ariel spun around like a miniature supermodel and basked under her father glowing praises. Try as she might, Madeline could no longer suppress the smile tugging at her lips.

Russ slept through intermission and the entire second half of the ballet, but his eyes still lit with joy when it was time to file out of the theater and he saw his father was part of the group.

"Dad, you came. Mommy didn't think you would."

Madeline groaned; traitors surrounded her.

"So I've heard." Russell laughed and ruffled his son's head. "We better get going, we still have reservations for dinner.

Madeline's night went from bad to worse. Not because Russell turned out to be an ass, but because he wasn't. In fact, he seemed to go out of his way to be the perfect father, doting and spoiling the children. The problem was he also went out of his way to ignore her.

He wasn't rude about it, but she still felt invisible. Why hadn't he commented about how good she looked or tried to make her laugh? And when Ariel expressed an interest in going ice-skating at Rockefeller Center, everyone seemed to forget that she was operating with just one good leg.

"If you want to go skating then that's what we'll do," Russell declared, and then turned to her. "We'll let Dennis take you home and then come back and get me and the kids."

Madeline blinked. She wasn't imagining things. He didn't want her tagging along. "Well, I don't mind going."

"Momma, you can't skate on a bad leg," Russ said as if she didn't realize the obvious.

"I know, but—"

"And you're in a gown," Ariel added.

It was official. None of them wanted her around.

"I do have, uh, an early meeting in the morning," she agreed, blinking back tears. "I guess I should crash early."

"Then it's settled," Russell said with a tight smile, and then returned his attention to the children.

At Rockefeller Center, it took everything Madeline had not to beg to tag along as part of this bonding experience. But in the end, everyone filed out of the limo without a backward glance.

"I'm losing my babies," she whispered as Dennis pulled away from the curb.

"Ma'am?" Dennis asked.

Madeline shook her head and wiped the tears from her face. "Nothing," she mumbled.

During the long ride back home, her emotions swung from anger, hurt, jealousy and annoyance. What right did Russell have to brush her aside? She hadn't done anything to him. What happened to their truce?

The house seemed eerily quiet and way too

empty. She wondered if she would actually be able to get to sleep. Showering was an adventure with her cast foot, but afterward, she donned a lacy silk number and paced before her window waiting for Russell and the children to return.

"What if they like him more than me?" The question draped around her like a depressing blanket. Look what he'd been able to accomplish in such a short time.

Then something else occurred to her. What sort of custody battle should she expect when it came time for her to file for divorce?

The old Russell would have been too busy partying to fight for full custody. This new Russell just might give her the fight of her life.

"Damn it!" She turned from the window. "Why didn't I think of this before?" Was that why he'd mentioned divorce this past weekend? Why had he asked about why she'd married him?

Christopher.

She nearly laughed when his name floated across her mind. Her brother-in-law had not been pleased with Russell Stone's will, making her an equal partner in Stone Cold Records. If anyone would be happy to get rid of her, it would be him.

She turned from the window with her cane and

marched to the guestroom Russell was staying in. It was one of the larger rooms but as far as she could tell, he wasn't using up too much space.

In the closet, hung a few suits, undoubtedly what Christopher leant him, and at the bottom of the closet was an ugly leather duffel bag. She pulled it out, her mind awhirl with what secrets she'd find. At this point, she welcomed anything that would give her a better insight to her husband. As weird as that sounded.

But there was no jackpot to be found. All that was inside his duffel bag were a few jeans and T-shirts. There was a folder from the Shaw Agency with pictures and bios of each member of the family, but other than that, nothing.

Madeline sighed for coming up empty, but then heard something else in the bag. She picked up the bag, shook it and then commenced digging through the side pockets to get to the mysterious item. When she at last spotted a hole in the lining, she dug a finger inside and caught hold of a... ring?

"Madeline?"

Madeline jumped at the sound of Russell's voice and dropped the duffel bag back onto the bed.

Russell looked at her and then to the bag. "Mind telling me what the hell you think you're doing?"

"I was just, uh, I was just looking around," Madeline confessed the obvious.

"You mean, you were snooping," Russell corrected, moving into the room. "Did you find what you were looking for?"

Madeline reached for her cane and walked around the bed. "You can't blame me for being curious," she snapped.

"Can't I?"

"No." She stopped before him, reveling in the kinetic energy pulsing between them. "You moved into my house—"

"Our house," he said, interrupting her.

"And despite the fact of you looking and sounding like my husband. You sure as hell don't act like him," Madeline said.

"That's supposed to be a good thing, right?"

"No...yes...I don't know," she finally settled on saying. "It's just freaking me out. Okay? And don't think I don't know what you and Christopher are up to."

Russell eyed her suspiciously. "I'm almost afraid to ask."

"Oh, don't play dumb. It doesn't become you."

She headed for the door, but Russell's large hand wrapped around her forearm.

"Humor me and tell me what you're talking about."

"All this talk about why I married you and that little divorce bomb you dropped on me the other day. You rise from the dead and in ten days you want a divorce?"

"I never said I wanted a divorce."

"You've been thinking it, or what was up with you ignoring me all night?"

"I didn't… Well, I haven't exactly been feeling that you *want* to be married to me. I mean, we do sleep in two different bedrooms and you go out of your way not to be alone with me. Unless, your being in here in a sexy negligee is leading to some sort of peace offering?"

"In your dreams, Russell." She finally mustered the strength to jerk her arm from his grasp.

"Madeline," he called softly, and waited for her to face him again. "In the past we might have agreed to a loveless marriage, but I won't agree to it this time around." He moved toward her, letting his words sink in. "We can stay together during the holidays, but if starting over isn't something you can do, come January one of us needs to file for divorce."

Chapter 17

Dark sky. Angry clouds. Falling—no, losing altitude—losing control. Smoke. He *could* smell smoke. Black smoke.

"Mayday! Mayday!"

His voice, a cry for help was clogged with fear. Twisting and clawing, Russell struggled to fight himself out the nightmare; however, the more he wrestled the further he slipped into the nightmare.

We're going down. Dear God, we're going down.

He tried to scream again, but now he couldn't

squeeze air through his lungs. Blood rushed and threatened to burst his eardrums while his body tensed in preparation for the inevitable impact.

Just when he knew the crash would happen his eyes snapped open.

Russell bolted up in bed, his chest heaved as if it struggled to keep his heart from escaping. His eyes darted around the darkroom. He could still smell the black smoke and he even tasted his own fear. After a long while, his brain recognized the guestroom and, more importantly, he remembered how he'd gotten there.

"Jesus," he groaned, dropping his head into the palms of his hands. Frustrated, he detangled himself from the bed's silk sheets and climbed out. In a strange way, the room's cold hardwood floor comforted him and grounded him back in reality.

A glance at the clock revealed he'd managed to steal a measly two hours of sleep, if one wanted to call tossing and turning sleep. Lately, he spent half his time covering the fact he was a walking zombie. He wasn't sure how much longer he could keep up the charade.

Sighing, Russell crept across the room to the adjoining bathroom and he quickly splashed cold water onto his face. Yet, when he peeked through his fingers at his reflection, he was stunned to see an image of his face in green-and-black paint. He gasped, blinked and his mirrored reflection returned to normal.

For a while, he was too stunned to move, but then his lungs demanded oxygen and he was forced to draw in air. He moved his hands along his face, watching his image do the same.

"I'm going crazy," he mumbled, and released an awkward laugh. At last, he turned out the light and left the bathroom before more strangers appeared in the mirror. One thing for sure, he wasn't going to be able to get back to sleep so he bypassed the bed and headed for the door.

Russell moved along the hallway of the museum he called a house, feeling like an intruder. Given how his own wife treated him, he might as well be one. He drew a deep breath, troubled by the perpetual stalemate of their marriage.

He didn't want a divorce, but what they had hardly qualified as a marriage. Unfortunately, the demise of their relationship obviously rested on his shoulders. Then again, if she only married him for the money…?

With a firm shake of his head, he tried to stop his thoughts from chasing each other, but it seemed like a habit he couldn't a break. Russell stopped before Ariel's bedroom and quietly opened the door. He didn't venture inside, but drew comfort from just seeing her small body nestled beneath her blanket.

His daughter was an absolute joy and he loved how she looked up to him with such trust and wonder. He couldn't imagine ever letting her down or not being her hero.

Russell closed the door and made his way to Russ's bedroom. He chuckled at the sight of his son curled up with his football. He could just imagine his son dreaming about running down a football field with fans cheering his name.

If there was anything that he loved about being Russell Stone, it was his children.

Closing the door, Russell turned around to face the bedroom at the end of the hallway. Madeline's bedroom. His overactive imagination went work. He could picture his hellcat of a wife in that sexy, silk number she'd had on earlier. Her hair was probably a tussled mess across an army of pillows and if he was lucky, she was dreaming about him.

The last part of that fantasy made him laugh. If anything, she was dreaming about throwing darts at his head. Though it was silly, Russell found himself walking toward the door. When he reached it, he drew several deep breaths before reaching for the doorknob.

He half expected, even hoped to find it locked, but then the knob twisted in his hand and he was in. *I'm just going to sneak a peek.*

Russell pushed open the door and entered. He walked what seemed like a mile across the plush carpet to the king-size bed. As predicted, Madeline's long mane of hair was spread across satin pillows. It was a bonus to see she'd kicked most of the covers off her body and her ample curves were on open display for his greedy eyes.

He watched her for a few minutes, not knowing what he'd say if she woke up. He shouldn't, but he sat down on the edge of the bed anyway and pushed back a few strands of hair and studied the details of her face for the bazillionth time in the last few weeks.

She truly was a beautiful, strong woman. In his absence, she'd done a hell of a job with the children and even with the businesses, though his brother would never admit it. And now*she was starting something on her own, an admirable feat for anyone.

He leaned down; unable to fight the urge to kiss her and even braced for an attack.

It didn't happen. Instead of fighting him, Madeline moaned in her sleep and actually kissed him back.

Despite the opportunity, he kept his hands at his sides, not daring to caress her inviting curves. To do so would have been a violation and there were already too many problems floating between them.

Somehow he found the strength to break the kiss and stood away from the bed.

"Russell," she whispered, and then rolled onto her side.

She is thinking about me. He smiled and backed out of the room. If he was lucky, he might be able to steal another kiss tomorrow night.

For the next two weeks Russell's threat of a divorce danced inside Madeline's head and she didn't breathe a word of it to her mother or her cousin, Lysandra. Strangely enough, Russell carried on as if the conversation never occurred. He continued to laugh and play with the children as if nothing was wrong between them.

Perhaps that was what hurt the most.

Every night she went to bed dreaming about him. Sometimes she woke and would almost swear the taste of him lingered on her lips. Those were the times she'd wake with her body pulsing with a need so strong, it took everything she had not to traipse down the hall to his room and…

Lord, I'm going crazy.

With Christmas just seven days away, the only question for Madeline was whether she wanted a new start with her husband. And if she did, would she be able to handle the evitable heartache?

The mornings when she woke to find him cooking breakfast was alarming since she had never known him to cook a day in his life. But now, French toast and seafood omelets were his specialties.

He didn't make it home by six every night, but when he couldn't, he always made it a point to call or check in. And without fail, he made sure to arrive in time for bedtime stories and to kiss his pumpkin good-night. A couple of nights, he arrived to tuck the children in and then went right back out for some business-related party, or another.

It pained her to admit it, but Madeline grew more jealous of Ariel with each passing day. And Russ now was in full hero worship of his father, begging to spend time with him at the studio or playing hours of video football.

Meanwhile, Madeline spent half her time telling herself that she still hated Russell and the other time convinced that she was falling in love with him. *Now, how crazy was that?*

"Maddie, are you even listening to me?"

Lysandra's voice broke through Madeline's deep thoughts and she blinked and glanced around her cluttered office. Hell, she'd forgotten where she was.

"Do you want to tell me what's going on with you?"

A derisive laugh tumbled from Madeline's lips. How could she tell when she didn't even know herself?

"Well?" Lysandra pressed.

A beep over her phone's intercom saved her from answering.

"Mrs. Stone?" her administrative assistant questioned.

"Yes, Kate?"

"Uh…receptionist just buzzed me. Your, uh, husband is on his way up."

Madeline's gaze flew to Lysandra. "What do you mean, he's on his way up?"

"He's in the elevator, supposedly carrying an armload of roses."

"Uh...thank you." Madeline stood, sat and stood again. "Wonder what he's doing here?" she whispered nervously.

"I was just about to ask you the same thing," Lysandra said. "What's going on with you two? Roses?"

"Nothing," she admitted, pulling open her desk drawer and grabbing her emergency compact to check her lipstick and smooth down the sides of her hair.

"I wouldn't believe it, if I wasn't seeing all of this with my own two eyes." Lysandra laughed.

Russell appeared in the outer offices, drawing every eye in the place toward him.

"You know, he's definitely sexier with that goatee he's sporting," Lysandra commented. "Maybe you should get him to model some of the men's clothes for our first fashion line?"

It actually wasn't a bad idea. Once again, Madeline's stomach looped into knots as she watched her husband stride toward her office. Besides the handsome face, he had wonderful broad shoulders, a lean frame and a confident gait.

Russell knocked on her glass door a second before opening it. "Am I interrupting?"

"Uh, no. Come on in." She fluttered a smile

and gestured to her cousin. "You remember Lysandra?"

"Of course." He nodded and entered the office with a lazy smile and then gestured to flowers. "I brought you a gift."

Madeline's eyes finally landed on the roses. "They're beautiful." She paused, but then finally had to ask. "What's the occasion?"

"No occasion. I figure a beautiful woman should always have beautiful flowers."

Lysandra smiled behind Russell's back and gave her cousin the thumbs-up.

Madeline tried to suppress a smile but failed miserably as she accepted the roses and inhaled their fragrant scent. "Thank you. They are very beautiful."

Russell's smile widened. "Can I steal you away for a quick lunch?"

"Lunch?" She blinked and glanced over at Lysandra.

"We can reschedule for another time. You go. I'll make your apologies to Cecelia."

"Are you sure?" Russell asked. "I don't want to impose."

"If she won't go with you, I will," Lysandra said.

"Ly!"

"What?" Lysandra feigned ignorance. "Do you even know the last time I had a lunch date with a member of the opposite sex?"

Russell chuckled. "Then I should be on the lookout for the perfect man for you," he said. "We have plenty of bachelors coming in and out of our doors over at the label."

"You'd fix me up on a blind date?" Lysandra asked with what sounded like awe tinged with gratitude.

"Of course," he said. "After all, we are family."

"Wow. You really are a changed man." She turned toward her cousin. "I guess I'll see you after lunch?" Lysandra gave Madeline a look that said that she expected to hear every juicy detail when they returned.

Madeline placed the roses on her desk and then reached for her cane. Russell retrieved her coat by the door and gently helped her into it.

This was the closest she'd been to Russell since their talk in his bedroom a couple of weeks ago and she found herself basking in his scent and once again enjoying the energy pulsing between them. For some reason her eyes settled on his thick lips and she suddenly longed to feel them pressed against hers.

How would he react if she initiated a kiss? Would he laugh or return it? And if he did either, how would she react?

Russell opened the office door for her and now both of them were the center of attention as the walked through the outer offices and down the long hallway. It wasn't until after they had left the building that Madeline thought to make introductions.

"What's wrong? Did you forget something?" Russell asked when she stopped in the middle of the sidewalk.

"Um, no." She waved her absent mindlessness away and pulled her coat tighter around her body. "It's still snowing out here." She tilted up her head and enjoyed the cool air blowing against her face. On impulse, she opened her mouth and tasted a few snowflakes.

She opened her eyes to see Russell watching her with open fascination. "What?"

He smiled with a casual shrug. "I like it when you're not always on guard."

"I'm not," she said.

"Yes, you are." He offered her his arm.

She hesitated, feeling that something was changing between them. Even now, it was hard to let the past go. It was even harder for her to admit to herself that she wanted a new beginning with this new Russell.

"We'll look pretty stupid standing out here the entire lunch hour," he said, flashing his dimples, actually, one dimple. Not two.

Madeline cocked her head, thinking, but finally slid her arm through his. What the hell? What did she have to lose?

Just your heart.

She drew a deep breath and glanced around for the limo. "So…where are we going?"

Russell lifted his free arm and waved to someone down the busy street. "I figured I'd take you to one of your favorite Italian restaurants."

Her eyebrows rose high with curiosity. "You remembered my favorite restaurant?"

"I, uh, no." He smiled sheepishly. "I asked Consuela. She's a wealth of information. I hope she signed a confidentially agreement, because if she ever wrote a book…"

"You've been pumping her for information about me?" she asked flattered.

"I had to ask someone." His eyes twinkled as a white carriage pulled up to the curb.

Madeline blinked and glanced around. "It's a little cold for an open carriage, don't you think?"

"I guess we'll have to snuggle close to keep warm." He opened the carriage door. "After you, ma'am."

She laughed at his chivalry and teased, "I don't know what you did with my old husband, but I think I like you a lot better."

"Good." Russell winked. "I like you a whole lot, too."

Chapter 18

Christmas morning, Madcline woke to the sound of her children tearing into her bedroom, begging for her to get up. She groaned and gave them the same line they gave her each morning when it was time to get up for school. "Oh, five more minutes." She rolled onto her side, hiding her smile in the pillow.

"No, no. Please get up," Ariel begged. "Daddy says we can't open our gifts until you wake up."

"Five more minutes," she whined again.

"Moooomm," Russ and Ariel chorused.

"Are you two in here bothering your mother?" Russell's commanding baritone sliced into the room and effectively ended the children's complaining.

Madeline's smile grew wider at her and Russell's well-rehearsed script.

"C'mon out. Let your momma get some sleep."

"Aw, man," Russ whined. "What if she sleeps all morning?"

It was hard, but Madeline swallowed her laughter and listened as her precious babies dragged out of her room. Once Russell closed the door behind them, she tossed back the covers and quickly climbed into her wheelchair.

She cracked open the door, peek out and burned rubber toward the service elevators. Even with Russell's promises to stall on the staircase, Madeline had just managed to reach the large Christmas tree downstairs when he and the children entered the room.

"Mommy!" Ariel exploded into the room... not to hug her mother, but to dive for the gifts underneath the tree.

Madeline laughed and commenced taking pictures while Russell manned the camcorder. Within minutes the floor was covered with ripped Christmas paper, bows and discarded open boxes.

The children's face lit up with each gift an Madeline was impressed with Russell's selections of baby dolls, PlayStation games, dresses and football jerseys.

"Consuela?" she asked.

"No," he shook his head proudly. "I was able to figure these out all on my own," he said.

She nodded, happy that her gifts of cameras, computers and autographed footballs were also great hits.

Then came the awkward moment when Ariel raced to her father, carrying a gift.

"Daddy, this one is for you."

Russell lowered the camcorder. "For me?"

Madeline also lowered her camera while she tried to get a handle on her nerves. However, she was unprepared when Russ ran to her carrying a box.

"Mommy, this one has your name on it."

"Me?" she echoed, and glanced back up at Russell.

The children returned to their gifts while Russell and Madeline carefully opened their own.

Russell was the first to get his opened. Puzzled, he pulled out a long silver chain. At the end was a set of dog tags.

Madeline flashed a timid smile. "It's sort of a joke," she offered apologetically. "A bad one."

Russell turned the tags over in his hand and read his name; but he felt something else. Déjà vu?

"I figured, it would come in handy if you ever got lost again," Madeline went on. When he didn't say anything, she assumed that he didn't like it. "I'm sorry. I just didn't know what else to get you."

Still, he kept flipping the tags over in his hand.

Sighing, Madeline finally opened her gift. It was her turn to be puzzled when she pulled out a thick set of papers cut in half, but then she recognized them. "Our prenuptial agreement?"

Russell blinked out of his trance. "I, uh, got them from my attorney. He still had a set of them filed away."

"But it's cut in half?" She looked back up at him, still unable to figure it out.

"It's null and void," he said.

"W-what?"

"It seems only right." He shrugged. "If this doesn't work out…" He dropped his gaze. "And I'm hoping that really won't be the case…you deserve half."

Madeline was speechless. Sure, the past week

with Russell had been wonderful. He'd shown up at her office everyday to take her out to lunch. He even seemed interested in the ins and outs of House of Madeline.

The interest also floored her since the old Russell believed a wife's place was at the home, except for the few occasions when they are invited out as arm candy.

"I don't know what to say," she admitted. "I'm overwhelmed."

Russell wanted to add that he'd annulled the prenuptial agreement mainly because he didn't want her to stay simply for the money. Of course, Christopher would have a fit when he found out, but this was something that needed to be done. If there was a chance for him and Madeline, he wanted her to stay because she loved him and not because of his money.

It was a big risk, but one that needed to be made if they were to have any sort of future.

"Thank you," she finally said. Then came the tears. With the prenuptial agreement voided, there was no longer a threat to House of Madeline's financing. There was also no reason for her to stay in the marriage.

That was a reason to celebrate.

That should've made her happy.

But it didn't.

The rest of the morning passed in a blur with Ariel's Woody Woodpecker laughs and Russ's engaging everyone in at least one of his new video games. In the afternoon, Christopher and Tiffani made their appearances and handed out even more gifts to the children.

Even after Cecelia and Lysandra showed up, Madeline's thoughts were still reeling from Russell's Christmas gift.

At last, while she was changing in her bedroom, Madeline showed her mother and Lysandra what had rendered her speechless.

"Well, I'll be damned." Cecelia collapsed on the bed. "You still have the Midas touch. Maybe I should start taking lessons from you."

Madeline rolled her eyes and limped over to the bedroom window to watch Russell, the children and Christopher create a snowman in between snowball fights. "Where does he get all his energy from?"

"That depends," Lysandra said, joining her at the window. "Are you still sleeping with Ariel at night?"

"What?" Cecelia jumped up from the bed. "He

tore up the prenuptial agreement and you're not even sleeping with him?"

"What can I say?" Madeline continued to watch Russell. "He's a changed man."

Russell took a snowball in the face and collapsed back against the snow-covered lawn. The children laughed and giggled in the distance while Christopher shouted a triumphant, "Bull's-eye!"

Russell chuckled, wiped the snow from his face and noticed that he had the perfect view into Madeline's window. She smiled and shook her head, but then finally gave him a small wave. Despite the cold December wind, the sight of her warmed Russell from the inside out.

By nightfall, the cold and wet gang trudged into the house to be spoiled by mugs of hot chocolate around a crackling fire.

Christopher slapped his hand across his brother's back. "Russell, I have to tell you this has been the best Christmas since…"

Everyone waited for him to finish the sentence, but when it became apparent that he couldn't, Russell returned the hard slap on the back and then squeezed Christopher's shoulders with affection. "I had a great time, too."

"I wish I could say the same," Tiffani mumbled, bored. "Can we go now? We promised my cousin we would stop by."

Christopher rolled his eyes, but said, "Of course, dear. Good night, everyone. Merry Christmas." He kissed his niece and nephew good-night, started toward Madeline but she smote him with a look that caused him to toss up his hands in surrender instead. "Take care, Madeline."

"You do the same." She folded her arms across her chest and was happy to watch him go.

After the guests were gone, Russ and Ariel started complaining at bathtime and continued until well after they were tucked in for the night.

"Go to sleep now and you can play with your toys in the morning," Madeline promised.

Ariel pouted despite the fact that she could barely keep her eyes open.

"Good night, baby." Madeline kissed her daughter's chubby cheeks and then headed for the door.

"Momma?"

"Yes, baby?"

"Are you and Daddy going to get a divorce?"

Madeline's heart plunged, but she managed to walk back over to the bed. "Why do you ask that?"

Ariel didn't answer.

"Sweetheart?" Madeline sat on the edge of the bed and brushed a few strands of hair from her daughter's face. "Did your father say something about a divorce?"

Ariel shook her head.

Madeline sighed in relief though she realized she shouldn't have been surprised by the question. Ariel and Russ were smart. They were bound to question why their parents slept in different bedrooms or for that matter showed no physical affection for one another. "Sweetheart, you don't need to worry about this. Your father and I...we're not getting a divorce."

Chapter 19

"Mayday! Mayday!"

Russell struggled to wake from the nightmare, again.

Dear God, we're going down.

Damn.

It was the same dream night after night. The same fear that made sleep impossible.

Frustrated, he detangled himself from the bed's silk sheets and climbed out. A glance at the clock revealed less than an hour's sleep.

In the bathroom, he splashed the customary

amount of water on to his face. His silver dog tags clanked against the sink and drew his eyes. He stood and dried his face before cupping and studying the tags. A memory tickled the back of his mind and he tried desperately to pull it to the forefront. After a few seconds, it just vanished.

Now he was exhausted *and* had a headache.

He grabbed a few aspirins from the medicine cabinet and swallowed the pills with a handful of water. "Get a hold of yourself, soldier," he mumbled under his breath, and hit the light switch on his way out of the bathroom.

Certain that sleep would once again elude him, Russell glided past the bed and crept out of the door to perform his nightly patrol to the children's bedrooms. Just remembering their excited faces on Christmas filled him with joy and he could hardly wait until next year.

When he turned toward Madeline's bedroom, his chest tightened and he had an instant erection. *I'll just look in on her.*

He entered the bedroom and walked quietly over to the bed. Like every night, Madeline's hair was spread over several pillows and she had kicked the covers off her body. Tonight, she wore a short, red silk negligee. Her long curvy legs seemed to go on forever and begged for his touch. Russell caressed one of them before thinking better of it. He glided his fingers along her soft flesh, his erection throbbed mercilessly and he fought the devil himself to prevent his hands from drifting higher.

He wanted to kiss her again, but experienced a tinge of guilt for stealing kisses in the middle of the night. Yet, he couldn't help himself. He pressed his lips against hers and her mouth parted to receive his probing tongue.

The sweet taste of her mouth left him light-headed while desire short-circuited his nerve endings. He imagined removing the silk negligee and touching every dip and curve of her body. He wanted to see what she'd look like in the throes of passion, hear his name as a passionate sigh from her lips and feel her body's warmth as she sheathed his throbbing erection.

Groaning, he lost track of his hand and it roamed high on her hips and then inched toward her panty line. Stop, he told himself. He had to stop. At last, he opened his eyes and stared straight into a field of green.

Russell broke away in alarm and stood away from the bed. "I'm sorry," he said, knowing how weak an apology it was, not to mention a big lie.

"I didn't…I didn't mean…" He walked backward toward the door, wondering whether she was thinking he was some type of sex pervert.

"Wait," Madeline said, stretching out a hand to him. "Don't go."

He stopped, not sure whether he'd heard her right.

"I don't want you to leave tonight," she said. She climbed out of bed and walked toward him with barely a limp. Her warm hand slid into his and she pulled him back toward the bed. "You come in here every night, don't you?"

Russell hesitated, but then finally nodded when the moonlight spilled across her face, giving her an angelic glow.

"Why?" she asked, sitting down on the bed and placing his hand against her breast.

He swallowed the sudden lump in his throat and relished the weight in his hand. "I like watching you," he admitted, and sat next to her.

She turned toward him, her warm breath brushed against his cheek. "Do you like kissing me, as well?"

She knows.

Russell's gaze lowered to her full lips. "I love kissing you."

Madeline slipped the spaghetti straps of her

To Love a Stranger

negligee off her creamy shoulders and Russell watched spellbound as the sheet of red silk fell and pooled at her waist. "Show me," she commanded softly.

The room seemed to fill with the sound of Russell's heartbeat as he leaned forward and claimed possession of her full lips.

She moaned and thrust her breasts against him.

Russell responded to the open invitation by cupping them both and giving them a hard squeeze. He pressed forward and leaned her back down into the pillows.

As he hovered beside her, Madeline's hand journeyed down the length of his body and then slid around his erection. His groan sounded like that of a wounded animal. He battled to gain control of his body, fearful that he would explode way before he truly got started.

His wife wasn't making it any easier with her slow, languid strokes and her lazy sighs of pleasure. Russell's kisses became soft nibbles. He sucked and bit at her lip, her long neck and then settled around one plump nipple.

Madeline gasped and arched her back. "Oh, God," she moaned, and increased the pressure around his swollen manhood. "Oh, Russell."

"Oh, baby," he panted, now blazing another trail down her flat belly, stopping briefly to dip his tongue inside her belly button.

Enjoying her body's tremors, Russell gently slipped her lacy panties off her bottom and glided them down her long legs, which opened without urging. Russell dove inside of her like a starving man, lapping and sucking at the pulsing rosebud at her center.

What Madeline felt went beyond pleasure and her ability to do the simplest things, like breathe, seemed impossible. She also couldn't hold still. By the time her first orgasm hit, her head was hanging over one side of the bed and her good leg had wrapped behind Russell's head. Still, his tongue plunged, rotated and plunged again, causing her second orgasm to hit before the first one finished quaking.

Russell could no longer stand the ache of the erection that tented his pajama pants. More than drunk from Madeline's sweet juices, he now needed to be buried in her silken walls. Pulling her body back to the center of the bed, he was surprised when she sat up and reached for the waist of his pants.

"Let me." Without waiting for a response, Madeline slipped her hands beneath the bands of his pajamas and pulled them down. Her eyes widened slightly at his thick hook-shaped erection.

Russell held his breath, waiting to see what she would do next. Just when he thought he couldn't take the suspense any longer, his wife leaned forward and kissed the tip of his manhood. One chaste kiss quickly turned into another and before long her mouth closed around his straining flesh.

"Mad…Maddie," he panted, closing his eyes. The slick walls of her hot mouth literally made his toes curl and tears leak from his eyes. "Oh, Maddie." He glided his hands through her hair and followed the hypnotic bob of her head.

More than once, she brought him to the brink, but then changed the rhythm to prolong the inevitable. Russell could only stand to be teased for so long. In one smooth move, he lifted and pinned her beneath him, stealing her breath with a long, deep kiss and easing into her body until he filled her completely.

Madeline trembled around him and Russell had to ground his teeth together while he once again stave off premature ejaculation. When he'd convinced himself that everything was under control, he moved with smooth, long strokes.

Soon, Madeline's hips matched him beat-for-beat, stroke-for-stroke and he was no longer capable of maintaining control.

"Oh, baby. You feel so good," he whispered into the crook of her neck, their tempo increasing by the seconds.

Madeline was incapable of responding. All she could do was bask in the pleasure he provided. Vaguely, she was aware of crying, but not from pain or sadness, but because she had never felt this wanton, this wild and this complete.

Feeling the beginnings of another orgasm, Madeline thrashed mindlessly while Russell's patient gentleness morphed into a desperate hammering. She dug her nails into the center of his back and locked her legs around his waist in order to hold on for the rest of the ride.

Madeline cried out as Russell growled and exploded inside of her. Panting, he pulled her close and then collapsed against her.

Sated, Madeline curled toward him and peppered his face with kisses. "That was wonderful."

"Yeah?" he asked, shyly. "I am a little out of practice."

"Trust me. You were perfect."

Russell cupped her breasts again. "Does that mean we get to do it again?"

She laughed. "As soon as I catch my breath."

He smiled lazily and then tilted her face so he could kiss her fully on the mouth. When he broke the kiss, she smiled back at him. "I may not remember how we met, or when we married," he said. "But I do know that I love you."

Touched by his words, tears shimmered in Madeline's eyes. "I love you, too," she said, and she meant it. Even though she knew without a doubt that the man lying beside her was definitely *not* her husband.

Chapter 20

Dark sky. Angry clouds. Smoke. He could smell smoke. Black smoke.

"Mayday! Mayday!"

We're going down. Dear God, we're going down.

He tried to scream but now he couldn't squeeze air through his lungs. Blood rushed and threatened to burst his eardrums while his body tensed in preparation for the inevitable impact.

A static voice buzzed in head. "What's your position, Maj. Cougar?"

Position. Position? He couldn't think. They were going to crash. The throttle of the helicopter rattled out of control in his hand while the static voice questioned him again. "What's your position, Maj. Cougar?"

"I-I-can't control it."

"Russell! Russell! Wake up!" Madeline shook his body, frightened that he was having some type of seizure. "Russell, please. You're scaring me," she said, desperate to wake him.

Russell continued to thrash and then suddenly his eyes snapped open. He bolted up in bed and Madeline released a startled cry of alarm.

"What?" He glanced around, and panicked when he was unable to recognize his surroundings. "Where am I?"

"You're in my room," the woman next to him answered in a small voice.

Wild eyed, he glanced over at her and then slowly relaxed as recognition settled in. "Madeline."

She flashed him a nervous smile, while her beautiful green gaze filled with questions.

"Bad dream," he answered the unasked question. "How long have I been asleep?"

"Quite a while. It's noon."

Russell blinked. "You're kidding?"

"No. Judging by the way you were snoring, I'd say you needed it." She laughed awkwardly.

"Oh, I'm sorry." He collapsed back against the pillows. "I've been having trouble sleeping." He tossed the covers back from his naked body and started to climb out. "Are the kids up?"

Madeline placed a staying hand against his shoulder. "Don't worry about them. They're playing at the neighbors. How long have you been having trouble sleeping?"

He couldn't answer the question. It seemed like forever. When he didn't answer, he saw worry lines etch into her face. "Don't worry I'm fine. I've been able to operate pretty good with just a few hours of sleep. Sometimes even less than that," he said.

His words of assurance had the opposite affect.

Madeline's gaze dropped to his naked body. "How did you get all these scars?" Her fingers traced a long jagged scar on his right side and then leapt to a few smaller ones on the left side. "You have a few keloids on your back, too."

"I don't know. It must have something to do with the crash."

Madeline removed her hand from his scar and glanced up to meet his questioning stare.

"Is something wrong, baby?"

How could she answer such a question? Everything is fine...except there's this naked stranger in my bed.

"What is it, baby? Why are you crying?"

Madeline touched her face, surprised there were, indeed, tears. "It's nothing. It's just that... last night was so beautiful."

Russell smiled and relaxed. "You mean, whenever I could keep you *on* the bed?"

Her cheeks burned with embarrassment. That had never been a problem for her in the past. But there was an intensity and an unbridled passion that had transferred between them last night that she couldn't hold still and truth be told, her body was aching for another round right now.

"How did you meet Shaw?" she asked instead.

"The detective?"

She nodded, keeping her gaze leveled with his to see if she could read the truth in his eyes. "It was pretty much like he said. At the hospital."

"Queen Elizabeth?"

Russell opened his mouth, closed it and wrinkled his forehead in deep thought. "Yeah." He gazed off into the distance for a long moment, and then shook his head as if the question had given him a headache.

Madeline's gaze dropped and again returned to the scars across his body. Something had happened to him; that was for sure. Then again, what about the blood test? How on earth did he pass a blood test?

"I'm starving. What about you?" Russell said, pulling her body against him. He sniffed the column of her neck and sighed dreamily. "You smell like baby powder. You've already hit the shower?"

"Well, we both can't lie in bed all day," she teased.

"Why not?" He slid up her pink chemise and exposed her full breasts. "The children are gone and neither of us has to go into the office today. We can play all day if we want to."

It was true, she realized. Last night, she had been too caught up in the heat of the moment, but now in the light of day, she knew that carrying on such a charade was wrong—wasn't it?

Russell's hot mouth locked around a pert nipple while his large hand slid down in between her legs. "Mmm. It seems as if you're ready to play," he said.

Madeline closed her eyes and panted, "I thought you were about to get up and get something to eat?"

"I don't have to get out of bed for that."

Her panties came off with a firm yank and Russell planted himself between her legs to prove his point.

The war between her head and her heart was probably the shortest war ever fought. There was something about the way his hands roamed over her skin, the way his mouth raised her body's temperature and just the beautiful way he made love to her that made her feel so complete.

By her second orgasm, Madeline's voice was reduced to a breathless pant and joyful tears rolled from her eyes and soaked her pillow. Even then, she didn't want him to stop. Heck, she never even wanted to leave the bed.

Sooner or later she would have to get answers—just not right now.

Russell burrowed deep into Madeline, relishing the way her slick velvet walls lulled him into a peaceful utopia. He loved the way her slim fingers rolled down his back and then settled against his butt in silent urging.

Madeline's sighs escalated and every muscle in her body tightened. He growled, knowing that she was on the verge of another orgasm. She was wet, slippery, warm and moist. Soon his own breathing came out in short sporadic puffs.

Madeline tossed back her hair and Russell watched, fascinated by her uninhibited response. Her contractions squeezed him and drove him insane. With each thrust, he lost a piece of himself, of his soul, to her.

A grand climatic cry tore from her long, smooth throat and he erupted soon after, his body quaking with violent, intense spasms.

"God, I love you." He rained kisses along the side of her face, down her neck and across her collarbone. He breathed in the musky scent of their lovemaking. "I love you."

She curled and snuggled against him and pressed a kiss against his sweat, slick forehead. "I love you, too."

Russell smiled and glanced up, but halted at the sight of her tears. "You're crying again." He gently brushed a them away. "Why the tears?"

Her smile flickered briefly. "Because I'm so happy." She gazed deep into his eyes. "You make me so happy."

"Then I hope that I will always make you this happy."

Madeline nodded, but in her heart, she knew this was one promise he couldn't keep.

The last few days of December flew by in a haze. The children continued their joyous bonding with Russell with plenty of snowballs fights, video-game tournaments and s'mores by firelight. Plus, they seemed giddy about the fact he'd finally moved into their mother's bedroom.

Madeline couldn't complain, either. Her nights and mornings were filled with wild, mind-blowing sex that she had only dreamed about. Every time she thought she couldn't possible stand another round, Russell wrangled another orgasm out of her exhausted body.

When they were having sex, Russell picked her brain about the ins and outs of her job and he really listened, questioned her ideas and encouraged her whenever she mentioned some particular difficulties she was having with distributors, model agencies or just simple fabric decisions.

Once he'd asked what had taken her so long to get started on her dreams and she had to refrain from telling him that he—or rather her real husband—had discouraged her from doing anything other than joining the right wives clubs and posing prettily for the cameras.

Christopher threw an outrageous New Year's Eve party at his estate and he immediately sensed that something had changed between Russell and Madeline and it made him nervous. Throughout the evening the two behaved more like newly-weds than two people who were on the verge of a divorce…like he'd hoped.

As a result, he hit the bar fast and furious. It didn't help that Madeline tried constantly to corner him.

Had she finally found out the truth?

If so, he had a lot of explaining to do.

Damn. Why didn't Madeline file for divorce like a good girl? Christopher slammed back another drink and then scanned the dancing crowd to see *his brother* laughing at something Madeline whispered in his ear. Christopher's heart squeezed.

The same face.

The same voice.

The same laugh.

But he was *not* Russell.

He had been a fool thinking he could pull this off. He was also desperate. So enamored with the similarities that, he convinced himself that he could have his brother back.

However, for the last six weeks the office had been buzzing about the changes in Russell. Where the real Russell had been loud and gregarious, this Russell was more quiet and introverted. The real Russell loved women—often. This Russell only had eyes for Madeline.

Party horns blared and Stone Cold Records newest artist that was working the crowd called for everyone's attention.

Tiffani clamped a hand around Christopher's wrist and dragged him toward the stage. Standing before the crowd, his wife grabbed the microphone and glanced at her watch.

"All right, everybody. It's almost that time to ring in the New Year!"

The crowd cheered.

Christopher caught sight of Russell and Madeline again. He was laughing. She was staring at Christopher.

She knows.

Tiffani began the countdown. "Ten, nine, eight…"

Christopher looked away and chiseled a smile on his face.

"Six, five, four…"

Watching her skittish brother-in-law, Madeline had her answer. And with the holidays drawing to a close, she had a serious decision to make. Uncover the truth about the stranger she had fallen in love with, or go on pretending the imposter was her husband.

"Three, two, one…Happy New Year!"

Glittering confetti, balloons and streamers fell on the exuberant crowd while several blasts from party horns rattled her eardrums.

Russell gathered her close, enveloping her with loving arms. "Happy New Year, sweetheart. I love you." He leaned forward and planted the sweetest kiss against her full lips.

I love you, too. Whoever you are.

Chapter 21

For the first time in a long while, Russell slept peacefully throughout the night. A great deal of that was attributed to the sex marathon he and Madeline competed in for the last week. He certainly wasn't complaining. Madeline's body was a wonderland of smooth curves, jasmine-scented valleys and warm silken caverns. He had been more than willing to lose his mind and soul exploring every inch of it.

The morning's bright winter sun bathed and warmed his body. With a great sigh, Russell stretched every muscle in his body. Was it possible to feel any more content than he did at this moment? Of course he could. He and Madeline could engage in one more round of lovemaking before having to get up.

Smiling, Russell slid his hands across the bed. "Baby," he purred. However, his hands never made contact with Madeline.

He snapped open his eyes and then bolted up in bed. However, he wasn't alone. Madeline sat curled up in the bedroom's window, watching him.

He laughed and then relaxed back against the pillows. "What are you doing over there?" Russell patted the empty spot beside him. "Why don't you come back to bed before we're rudely interrupted?"

Madeline's face flushed prettily and Russell was instantly hard again.

"Or," he said, climbing out the sheets, "I can join you over there."

"No. No." She threw up her hands, though a smile still hung on her lips. "Stop," she said.

"Why?" He asked, standing nude from the bed.

"Because."

"Because why?" he asked, sounding eerily like their eight-year old. Russell reached the window, swept her into his arms and pressed a fervent kiss against her lips.

They moaned together as Madeline leaned slack against him. The feel of her hard nipples against his chest caused Russell's heart to ram full throttle against his chest.

When his lungs finally demanded oxygen, he broke the kiss, but still kept their foreheads pressed together.

"Because I said so," she whispered finally. "I can't think when you do that."

He chuckled and peppered kisses across her closed eyelids. "Don't think. Feel." He inhaled the soft fragrance of her hair and roamed his fingertips lightly down curves of her body. "Can you feel me?"

She moaned again and sighed. "Yes."

It was a good thing, but he was definitely feeling her, not just physically, but emotionally. They belonged together. It was the one thing he was sure of. He saw them having more children and growing old together.

A part of him didn't care whether his memory returned because he was no longer the man people talked about. He had no desire to stay out at clubs all night, drape himself with obnoxiously sized diamonds or compete with Christopher on the amount of notches to add on his bedpost.

After work, all he wanted to do was stay home and spend time with Madeline and the children. It sounded cliché, but home really was where his heart lay.

"I have an idea," he said, stealing a quick kiss.

She lifted her adorable green eyes and stared into his soul.

"Let's get married," he whispered excitedly. To his surprise, she stiffened in his arms. "I know that we're already married but...I'm not that same man." He stroked a hand through her hair. "And I have a feeling you're not the same woman."

"Russell, I-I..."

"We can do it right here at the house. Ariel could be the little flower girl and Russ could be the ring bearer or the best man. Although, he'd probably have to fight his Uncle Chris for that privilege."

Madeline shook her head and pressed against his chest. "Whoa, whoa. You're moving too fast here." She succeeded in escaping his embrace and turning her back toward him.

Confused, Russell felt as if a steel vise had clamped around his heart. Had the last six weeks, heck, the last week meant nothing? Now that the holidays were over, had she planned to take him up on his offer for a divorce? He braced himself, suddenly feeling sick.

"What's the matter, Pamela? Don't you love me?"

Madeline whipped around. "Who's Pamela?"

Russell blinked. Had he said Pamela? "I-I don't know." But he did know, didn't he? He tried concentrating on the name, but after a moment, his head exploded with pain.

"Here, here. Come lie down." Madeline helped him over to the bed and then limped to the bathroom for a bottle of Tylenol and a glass of water. "Hold on, let me go get you some crackers or something."

Despite the pain and discomfort, Russell rather liked being taken care of by Madeline. Seeing her fuss over him put his fears to rest. She loved him. It was in everything she did.

"How are you feeling?" she asked, once the pain began to subside.

"I'll feel better when you agree to marry me."

Her shoulders deflated and she started to turn away from the bed.

Russell reached out and caught one of her wrists.

Madeline glanced back down at him.

"Say 'yes,'" he urged, and then pulled her down to lay beside him in bed. "Say 'yes.'" He curled toward her and once again rained kisses on her face, all the while urging her to, "Say 'yes.'"

Seconds later, the word *yes* fell from her lips and Russell made love to the woman who held his heart completely.

The first business day of the New Year, Christopher returned to work. It was before nine o'clock but he had already downed half a bottle of Crown Royal in preparation for the day ahead and a possible confrontation with Madeline. He didn't know what time she'd show up...he just knew that she would.

Lucky for him, he didn't have too long to wait. His secretary announced her arrival a few minutes after nine. He could have stalled, constructed some lie, but he wouldn't be able to avoid her forever.

"Send her in." Christopher sat back in his chair and braced himself for the worst.

The door opened and Madeline glided in, looking the part of a fashion diva and glaring at him as though ready to eat him alive. "Christopher."

"Madeline. Won't you have a seat?"

"I'd rather stand."

He nodded and reached for his drink again. "To what do I owe this pleasure?"

She ignored the stupid question, but patiently crossed her arms and waited for him to stew in silence.

He didn't last longer than a few seconds. "I guess you want to talk about Russell."

"No. I want to talk to you about the stranger living under my roof, playing father to my impressionable children and…" She stopped and drew a deep breath to collect herself.

Christopher guessed what she wanted to say. "I figured that's how you found out."

In a blink of an eye her face turned to stone and she came close as humanly possible to breathing fire. "You figured that's how I'd find out? You purposely sent a stranger to my bed? Are you out of your mind?"

He worked his jaw, swallowed. "Maybe."

Madeline stared, shaking her head. "Why? Why would you lie?"

Christopher's eyes widened, incredulous. "Why do you think?" He finally stood from his chair, walked over to the window and gaze out at the skyline. "Look at him. He's a perfect carbon copy of Russell. His face, his voice and even his laugh." Tears raced down Christopher's face. "I just wanted my brother back."

Madeline walked stealthily to the window, but paid no attention to the view. "That's bull and you know it."

Christopher turned and locked gazes.

"You wanted your *damn* company back. Announce to the world that your dearly departed brother has returned from the dead, reinstate our prenuptial agreement and convince *Russell* to divorce me and—what? Were you hoping the man would never get his memory back? Hope that he would live the rest of his days as your long-lost brother? What?"

"You got it all wrong."

She stalked toward him. "You look me in the eyes and tell me none of this crossed your mind. Tell me you weren't behind him telling me to stick the marriage out until after holidays and then we should look into getting a divorce!"

Christopher opened his mouth, the denial seconds from falling off his tongue...but then he quickly closed his mouth and dropped his gaze.

Madeline reared back a fist and threw her

whole body into a punch across his jaw. Christopher's head rocked to the side. This time his body turned to stone and anger blazed in his eyes. Yet, his hands stayed clenched at his sides.

"Tell me, *Saint* Madeline. When did you discover he wasn't Russell? Last night?"

Madeline's gaze faltered.

"The night before?"

She clenched and unclenched her jaw.

"Tell me, what took you so long to confront me about this?"

Madeline moved from the window, but Christopher stalked behind her. "You *wanted* him to be Russell every bit as much as I did. You want him to be your husband. You want him to be the father of your children."

She whirled toward him. "Only because he's a better *man* than your brother ever dreamed of being."

"Face it. You just don't want to lose him."

"What makes you think I'll lose him?"

Christopher's lips sloped into an uneven line before he marched over to his desk and picked up a thick manila folder.

Dread seeped into Madeline's bones. She suddenly didn't want to continue this argument—

an argument it took her a week to prepare for. "What's that?"

"One guess."

She clutched her cane and hobbled backward toward the door, but Christopher reached her with lightening speed.

"You want the truth?" He shoved the folder into her arms. "Well, here you go, my dear. Peruse at your leisure."

The folder felt heavy, too heavy, in her arms. She willed herself not to look down at it. "How did you get this?"

Christopher laughed and walked over to the bar and poured himself another drink. "Care to join me?"

"Answer the question."

He took his time refreshing his drink and by the time he faced Madeline again, tears had worked their way up and blurred her vision.

"Dr. Rountree took not only his blood samples, but fingerprints. I contacted a few friends, greased a few pockets and—*voila.*"

"Fingerprints?" Madeline felt sick. "Please don't tell me he some kind of criminal. This all hasn't been some kind scam, has it?"

Christopher took a hefty swallow of his drink.

"No. As far as I can tell his memory loss is legit."
He watched as her shoulders slumped in relief, but
then continued studying her while she warred
with herself to read the information he'd given
her. "You're in love with him, aren't you?"

Madeline couldn't bring herself to answer. The
folder was getting heavier by the second. This
was her reward for not sticking to her mother's
creed of falling for money and not love. Love
hurts a hell of a lot more.

"I'm sorry, Madeline," Christopher said, and
actually managed to look genuine in his apology.
"His name is Marcellus Cougar. Once Major Marcellus Cougar of the United States Army…and he
has a family…and a wife."

The folder slipped from her hands and crashed
to the floor. "He's married?"

Chapter 22

Madeline didn't remember leaving Stone Cold Records, driving to the House of Madeline or even how long she'd been staring out of her office window. One thing for sure, she hadn't mustered the courage to read Russell, or rather Marcellus's file. At the moment, she kept waiting for Christopher's words to stop ringing in her ear.

"Maddie?" Lysandra poked her head inside the office. When Madeline turned from the window, Lysandra's mouth dropped open. "My God. You look like… What's wrong?" She entered the office and closed the door behind her.

Madeline shook her head, prepared to lie through her teeth if need be, but one look at Lysandra's concerned face and she broke down.

In a flash, Lysandra enclosed her in her small embrace and, despite not knowing the problem, assured her cousin that everything was going to be all right.

"It's never gong to be all right," Madeline sobbed, clutching her cousin tight. "Everything is a mess. What am I going to do? What am I going to tell the children?"

"Okay, now you're scaring me. Come over here and sit down."

Madeline allowed her cousin to lead her over to her desk.

"Now. Tell me. What's going on? What happened?"

"Russell…I mean, Marcellus—he's not him. He's not mine. He can never be mine. I have to tell him. I have to let him go."

Lysandra knelt in front of Madeline, shaking her head. "Who? I don't understand. What did this guy do?"

Madeline turned and grabbed the folder. "It's in here. I can't make myself read it." She shoved into Lysandra's arms and then grabbed a few

Kleenexes to mop her tears. "You read it. You tell me what it says."

Lysandra still struggled to understand Madeline's babble, but she did glance down and read the name on the folder. "Marcellus Cougar." Her gaze found Madeline's again. "Who is he?"

Madeline fought for control of her trembling lips. "He's Russell." When no bells and whistles went off, she continued. "The new Russell…the one who's been living with me."

"You mean…Russell is not Russell?"

Hearing the truth like that caused a fresh wave of tears to rush down Madeline's face.

"But I don't understand." Lysandra opened the folder and pored over the numerous pages. "Here's a copy of a military ID, driver's license, and… How did you get all this?"

"Christopher," Madeline said both angrily and wearily. "He's known the whole time."

"What? Did you kill him?"

"No. Although, the thought did cross my mind."

"You want *me* to go kill him?"

"Tempting, but no. I have a much bigger problem on my hands. Like telling the kids… and Marcellus." She sighed. "Marcellus. It sort of suits him, don't you think?"

"Wait a minute? Christopher pulls an outrageous stunt like this and expects you to clean it up?"

"He doesn't want to give Russ—I mean, Marcellus—up. For him, it would be like losing his brother all over again." Madeline dropped her gaze. "I don't want to give him up, either."

Lysandra's concern collapsed into pity. "Oh, Maddie."

Madeline returned to her cousin's embrace and cried until the well ran dry.

Russell spent the morning in Tiffany's, searching for a wedding ring. When he first walked through the door, the saleswoman, Helen, presented one monstrous diamond after another. But he didn't like any of them.

"Something simple," he finally told the woman. "Simple yet elegant."

"More like an antique design?" Helen suggested, seeming impressed and pleased that he wasn't a man who just asked for the biggest diamond they had.

"I want a ring that reflects the qualities I love about her. Her intelligence, the way she dotes on my children and the subtle ways she shows her love for me. Nothing flashy or over the top."

Helen sighed dreamily. "She must be one hell of a woman."

Russell smiled. "She is."

"I don't think I've ever seen a man of your stature blush before."

"That's because the other men don't have a woman like mine," he said.

Helen winked. "I think I have the perfect ring for you."

And the perfect ring she had. It was an antique Asscher-cut diamond and platinum ring. The diamond's small table, high crown, deep pavilion and square culet gave it an almost octagonal appearance.

"Asscher-cut diamonds were developed in the early 1900s by the Asscher Diamond Company in Amsterdam," Helen went on to tell him. "They are extremely rare and desirable."

Russell's smile bloomed. "I'll take it."

Ten minutes later Russell headed back to his limo, feeling like the luckiest man on earth. He was already dreaming of ways to present the ring to Madeline: a fancy dinner, carriage ride through Central Park, or before a nice crackling fire.

Just like Pamela.

Russell stopped. Something ghosted around his memory or someone—a woman. He stood still in the middle of Fifth Avenue, the January wind freezing him to the bone.

Dennis frowned while still holding open the limousine door. "Did you find what you needed, Mr. Stone?"

Russell snapped out of his reverie, the ghost gone. He looked around the busy street, momentarily confused. His gaze searched the faces of the busy New Yorkers. None of them paid him any attention.

"Mr. Stone?" Dennis asked.

Russell didn't answer.

"Mayday! Mayday!"

"Mr. Stone?"

"What's your position, Major Cougar?"

"Mr. Stone?"

"What's your position?"

Dennis approached, concerned etched in his features. "Mr. Stone, are you all right?"

Russell touched the side of his head and felt the scar buried beneath his short-cropped hair.

"Do you need me to take you to the hospital, Mr. Stone? You don't look too good."

At long last, the men's gazes connected.

Russell blinked, shook his head and gave the young driver a reassuring smile. "Fine. Everything is fine." He pounded Dennis on the back for good measure. "Why don't we just go home?"

"You're not going into the office today?"

"No. I, uh, I'm going to take the day off."

"You're the boss."

Russell walked over to the limo and slipped inside. The moment the door closed behind him, he slumped back against the leather interior and tried to recapture the voice and images from moments ago.

Dennis slid behind the wheel and they melted back into traffic. Usually, the two engaged in friendly conversation during their drives, but after a couple of failed attempts, Dennis left his employer alone with his thoughts. However, he did keep watching him through his rearview mirror.

After a few intense minutes of heavy concentration, Russell felt the tingling of another headache. He abandoned his efforts and turned toward the limo's dark windows. The passing scenery calmed him, but then suddenly everything seemed wrong or rather something was missing.

"What's going on here?" he asked.

"Sir?"

Russell nodded to the massive construction site. "What are they working on?"

"The World Trade Center Memorial. It looks like it's coming along pretty good."

Something clicked inside Russell's head. "The World Trade Center...9/11."

Dennis's gaze snapped back to the mirror. "You remember the attacks, sir?"

"Oh, my God," Russell whispered.

"Sir? Are you all right? You look as though you've seen a ghost."

"Pull over, Dennis."

"Yes, sir."

"There's a lot in here," Lysandra said as she continued to pore over Marcellus Cougar's file.

Madeline snatched the last tissue from the box and returned to pacing the office. "All right. I can't stand it anymore." She marched over to her desk and plopped into her chair. "Just tell me what it says." She jumped back up. "Wait, no. Don't tell me." She returned to pacing.

Lysandra turned toward her cousin. "Look, Maddie. I know this has to be incredibly hard... but he's not a puppy. You can't keep him."

"Why not?" Madeline asked. "Just the three of us know the truth."

Lysandra cocked her head in weary sympathy. "Maddie."

"I know," she whined. "It's just that…he's so perfect. The kids love him."

"And you love him."

"Yes, damn it. I love him. Why do you think I'm losing my mind here?" Madeline swore under breath. "It's bad enough that I've know for over a week that he wasn't my husband. Russell wished he was that good in bed. Quantity doesn't mean quality."

"That good, huh?"

"Oh, Lysandra." She sighed almost dreamily. "He's attentive, eager to please and my God, he's like the Energizer bunny."

Lysandra's shoulders drooped. "Okay. Now I'm jealous."

"It never entered my mind that he had another wife somewhere."

Her cousin closed the folder. "You know what? I think you need to take this folder to Marcellus and you guys read it together."

"Then what? Watch him walk out the door?"

"I'm afraid so."

Madeline's lips trembled as fresh tears found their way to the surface.

Lysandra stood, walked over to her and placed the folder in her hands. "Just make sure you get a kiss goodbye."

There was a knock at the door.

Madeline groaned. She and Lysandra spent most of the day telling employees they were not to be disturbed. So when Madeline rounded toward the door to give whoever it was a piece of her mind, she was not prepared to see Marcellus.

Belatedly, she remembered to speak. "Oh, hi."

"Hello. Uh, Kate wasn't at her desk so I thought it was okay to come on in." He glanced over at Lysandra. "Is this a bad time?"

"Yes."

"No," Lysandra corrected. "I was just leaving."

Madeline's gaze cut to her traitorous cousin, but Lysandra was smart enough not to look in her direction. Both Madeline and Marcellus watched her as she left the office.

When they were finally alone, Marcellus turned to Madeline and took in her puffy, red eyes and disheveled appearance. "Is something wrong?" he asked, moving toward her.

"No, well, I'm fine," she said, stepping back

and sliding the folder behind her back. In order to think, she couldn't stand too close to him. "What are you doing here?"

For the first time, she noticed his drawn appearance, his troubled eyes.

"Have you talked with Christopher?" she asked fearfully.

"No. I didn't make it into the office today." He frowned. "Why?"

"No reason," she covered, and relaxed a little.

"Madeline, we need to talk."

The seriousness of his tone quickened her heartbeat and she finally read the truth in his eyes.

He knows.

"I don't know how to say this," he began.

"Then don't," she said without thinking. Her body showed no signs of running out of tears.

"You know, don't you?" he asked, strolling up to her.

She nodded though her vision was completely blurred.

"How…?"

"The first time we made love. It was also when I knew beyond a shadow of a doubt that I was in love with you."

Tears glistened in Marcellus's eyes. "I have to go."

"I know," she croaked. Dropping the folder, Madeline completely broke down.

Marcellus was at her side in a flash, pulling her into his strong embrace and whispering words of comfort. None of them worked.

Just make sure you get a kiss goodbye.

And that's exactly what she did.

Chapter 23

Ariel cried for a week.

Russ simply stopped talking.

After two months of the media raking him over the coals, Christopher Stone woke the morning of March first and put a bullet through his head. Three days later, after the funeral, Tiffani inherited a small sum and the rest of Christopher's estate was divided between Madeline and her children.

"Hot damn," Cecelia popped the cork off a bottle of champagne. "I never thought I'd be happy of the day you didn't listen to me." She quickly poured the gushing, bubbly into two flutes. "Just don't go around making it a habit."

"Mother, not now." Madeline removed her black hat and veil and then kicked her pumps across the room. "I never wanted his money and I have no clue how to run all these businesses."

"It's simple. You hire people."

Madeline sighed. Why did she even bother discussing this with her?

"Of course, this also means you're back on the market."

"Mother, if you mention Toby McDaniel. I swear, I'll scream."

Cecelia rolled her eyes and handed her daughter her flute of champagne. "There's that tone." She waved a slender finger in reprimand. "Besides, Toby is no longer available. I hooked him up with someone else already."

Madeline arched an inquisitive brow and set her champagne down on her vanity without a sip. "Who?"

Her mother fluttered a hand around. "Oh, just an acquaintance."

"Does this acquaintance have a name?"

"Denitra Bell," Cecelia mumbled into her glass.

The name was familiar and it took Madeline a

moment to place it. "That private eye's girlfriend? The one you called a Spandex Queen?"

"Yes, well, it turns out all she needed was some polishing."

Dubious, Madeline leveled her with a look.

"Okay. It took some major overhauling." Cecelia squared her shoulders. "But it was nice having a eager student. And if you ask me, it's way past time to enroll Ariel into charm school."

"Then it's a good thing nobody asked you."

There was a soft knock before Lysandra entered the room, as well.

"Now, *this one* I'd like to get my hands on."

"What?" Lysandra asked, suspicious she'd been the butt of a joke.

"Trust me. You don't want to know."

Lysandra took her at her word and informed them, "The kids are taking their naps."

"Thank you. Losing their uncle like this on top of…" She sighed. No matter what, Madeline's thoughts traveled back to Marcellus and, shortly after, her body ached from his absence. "I had no idea Christopher was suicidal. I knew he was taking the scandal pretty hard but…"

Lysandra took Madeline by the hand. "Don't. It's not your fault."

"Lately it seems everything is my fault. And I don't know how to fix any of it."

That included her heart. The one thing she tried her entire life to protect was now shattered into a million pieces.

Lysandra walked over to the vanity and picked up Marcellus's folder. "You still have this?"

Madeline nodded. Hell, she had the whole thing memorized. Major Marcellus Cougar was born and raised in Seattle Washington. One sibling—a younger sister. His father died a war hero in Vietnam. His mother a school teacher. Not much information about his academia, other than he'd joined the ROTC, but Madeline suspected Marcellus was a good student. He joined the military the same year he married Pamela Cutler.

Pamela. Madeline shook her head. She had never been prone to jealousy, but thinking of the woman who now warmed Marcellus's bed threatened to do her in.

The report did have some major gaps. Like whether the two had children. Or what Pamela did for a living as they bounced from one military base after another.

The fascinating material revolved around Marcellus's medical discharge from the military.

During his extended deployment in the Middle East, he was a sole survivor of a Black Hawk crash that not only battered his body but doctors had diagnosed him with severe post-traumatic stress disorder.

PTSD answered the questions about Marcellus's insomnia, small bouts of depression and memory loss.

"Well, I say, good riddance to him," Cecelia said, pouring herself another drink. "I knew he was a fraud the moment I laid eyes on him."

Madeline and Lysandra rolled their eyes.

"I told you. You can't fake good breeding. All that rolling around in the yard. Just be happy you were too smart to let him in your bed."

Madeline and Lysandra's gazes crashed. Neither corrected Cecelia or mentioned the child growing inside Madeline's body.

"And don't think I bought that whole traumatic-stress nonsense."

Madeline closed her eyes and wished like hell she could put a muzzle on her mother.

"Now, I know that you weren't in love with the real Russell Stone, dear. But you can't say he wasn't a great provider. And really, that's all a woman needs in a man. You start caring, or worse, loving them…and it'll lead to disaster." Cecelia's voice quivered.

When Madeline glanced over at her. She was stunned to see tears shimmering in her mother's eyes. "Are you crying?" Had she ever seen her mother cry before?

"Ah." Cecelia waved the question off. "Silly emotions."

"You were in love once, weren't you?" Madeline asked, stunned.

Cecelia straightened her shoulders and knuckled away a tear. "Once. Which is why I've always warned you against it. Women…and our silly notions of knights in shining armor and our crazy nonsense of happily-ever-after. It should be against the law to read little girls fairy tales. They do more harm than good."

Madeline ignored her mother's bluster and pressed, "Who was he?"

More tears leaked from Cecelia's eyes and Madeline grabbed a few Kleenexes from her vanity table and handed it to her. "Who?"

"Your damn father, who else?" Her mother dabbed her eyes.

"My father?" Madeline knew close to nothing about her father. Only that he was some Cape Cod summer fling who conveniently forgot to mention he was married.

"I was young and dumb," she said, downplaying the experience. "It can never be said that I didn't learn my lesson."

Sighing, Madeline shook her head. "But I didn't learn mine. No, I was never in love with Russell...but I do love Marcellus. I know that he doesn't have all the qualities you expect out of a husband, but he had every quality that I wanted." Tears resurfaced in Madeline's eyes.

"He doesn't come from moncy or, as far as, I can tell, aspire to be the next gazillionaire. But there was no denying he had heart. He was patient, caring and loving. He's a man who walked into our lives and turned it upside down. And before we knew it, he was gone again.

"And you know what? I would give it all up for him to walk back into our lives. Walk in and call Ariel pumpkin or run around out side tossing the football with Russ. I want us all to gather around a fireplace and eat s'mores until it's running out of our ears. And for once I want the father to be in the room when I deliver our child."

Madeline watched Cecelia's eyes widen in horror. "But don't worry, it'll never happen." Before she knew it, she'd broken down again. However, this time, it was her mother's arm that comforted her.

Seattle, Washington

Marcellus placed flowers against the tombstone of his wife's empty grave and wiped at the silent tears. In the past two months, he'd suffered an incredible amount of guilt for having forgotten about his beautiful wife. Their life together, the dreams they shared and how they all abruptly ended during the 9/11 attacks.

Pamela had never even been to New York before, but she always wanted to go to Broadway, Central Park and wave a sign in front of Good Morning America. So for her thirtieth birthday, Marcellus bought two tickets: one for Pamela and one for his mother. He couldn't go because he had just received deployment papers for the Middle East.

They left on a Friday, called him all weekend about the shows they caught and then waved their signs with Al Roker Monday. Tuesday morning, they'd decided, to have breakfast at the Windows of the World restaurant at the World Trade Center.

Marcellus took his next batch of flowers and

placed them across the few remains of his mother. Burying both women had been one of the hardest thing he'd ever done in his life. That and trying to convince himself that it wasn't his fault they were gone. He bought the tickets. He sent them that week.

His baby sister, Valerie, had tried her best to help ease his guilt. But it hadn't worked. What had helped, at least for a little while, was transforming himself into some kind of superhero during his three tours in the Middle East. What some of the guys on his squad called bravery, Marcellus called a death wish.

And he nearly got it.

His Black Hawk was shot down by small arms fire. Out of seven soldiers aboard, only he survived. After his physical injuries healed, the psychological ones began to pile. Post- traumatic stress syndrome had been his diagnoses and one month later, he'd received a medical discharge from the military.

His sister had left the states, married a Canadian doctor in Nova Scotia. Being his last surviving family member, he went to see her— only to learn that she'd died in a car accident the year before. No one had contacted him.

Looking back on it now. Maybe receiving the news on his in-laws' front porch had finally snapped something within him while he walked along the Nova Scotia seashore. The lives he was responsible for continued to pile. And then this week, Christopher Stone's suicide sent him reeling once again.

For six weeks he had been Christopher Stone's long lost little brother. He'd liked the man though now he knew they were from two different classes, two different worlds.

Madeline belonged to that other world, as well. A woman of privilege and fierce ambition wouldn't want anything to do with a man who had nothing. Hadn't she admitted that she'd only married for money?

Hell, he didn't even have a life anymore.

Marcellus had debated on whether to attend Christopher's funeral, but knew the media still swarmed like flies around the family. His beard was growing in full now, his hair a little unruly. One thing for sure, he wouldn't be wearing any Armani suits again anytime soon.

Lowering his head, Marcellus waited for another wave of guilt. Why was he thinking about another woman while at his wife's grave? The guilt never came. It had been over six years since

Pamela's death and the pain of his loss seemed to have a weaker hold over his heart. Not that he didn't still love her, it's just that… maybe it was time to move on.

Maybe it was okay to fall in love again. It was just too bad, he could never cross back over to that other world. Never hold Madeline Stone in his arms, never kiss his pumpkin good-night or toss the football around in the yard with Russ.

But for one moment in time, he did all those things. And it had been one of the happiest times in his life.

April showers were more like torrential rain in New York. One night, Madeline and the children couldn't sleep. As a treat, Madeline suggested they gather around the fireplace and eat s'mores. It'd also helped sate her massive chocolate cravings. But instead of cheering the children up, it seemed to depress them more.

Marcellus's presence was sorely missed.

"Maybe we can invite his other family to come live with us?" Ariel suggested sheepishly.

Russ huffed. "Don't be ridiculous."

"Russ, don't talk to your sister like that," Madeline gently reprimanded.

"Well, it was a stupid suggestion," he complained.

Madeline's brows stretched high into her forehead to let her son know not to try her patience on this.

"He said that he would never forget how to come home again," Ariel complained pitifully.

"Baby, I'm so sorry but we've been over this. Marcellus was not your father. He just looked like him."

"Does that mean that he never loved us?"

"Oh, baby. Come here." Madeline stretched out her arms and Ariel found room on her lap. "I'm sure Marcellus came to care for us very much. In his own way. It wasn't his fault that he was sick."

"Because he had annameseah?" Ariel questioned.

"Yes, baby." Madeline finger combed her daughter thick locks. "You mustn't hate him. You must never hate him." She sniffed.

"I don't hate him," Ariel mumbled. "I just wish that he could be our daddy again."

Madeline smiled through her brimming tears. "Me, too, baby."

Russ stood and ran to his room.

Chapter 24

New York Fashion week

The House of Madeline's first fashion show was minutes away from curtain call and they were opening to a packed house. Photographers, critics, celebrities and the just plain curious had turned out and packed the place.

Despite being irritable, cranky and wishing her due-at-any-moment child would get off her bladder, Madeline painted on a smile and raced around models, makeup artists and stagehands like a madwoman.

"Shouldn't you be taking it easy?" Lysandra asked, trying her best to direct Madeline to a chair. "We agreed that I would take care of everything back here."

Cecelia rounded a stage corner with Ariel and Russ at her side, dressed to the nines in their own House of Madeline clothing.

"Oh, look at my little angels," Madeline cooed, and planted kisses against each of their dimpled cheeks. "You guys want to watch the show backstage with Mommy?"

"Cecelia said we get to be models," Ariel said, keeping to the rule not to call Cecelia *grandma* in public.

"That's right. At the end of the show, we will all walk out and wave to the audience with that little bow we practiced at home to thank everyone for coming."

Russ sighed and fingered his collar like it was choking him.

"You okay, baby?" Madeline asked, though she sensed he'd rather do anything other than stroll down a catwalk.

However, Russ nodded and chose not to complain.

"How about we all go out for some pizza or ice cream after this?" It was clearly a bribe.

"Can we have both?" Russ tested.

"Sure, why not?"

"Thirty seconds to curtain!" Their stage director announced.

"I better go take my seat," Cecelia said, and then met Madeline's gaze. "If I haven't said it before, I'm very proud of you."

Surprised, Madeline smiled. "Thanks, Mom. I can't tell you how much that means to me."

They hugged briefly and Cecelia rushed off just as the house lights dimmed and the music grew louder.

Marcellus had hoped to blend with the crowd at the House of Madeline fashion premiere. He still wasn't certain whether it was actually a good idea to attend, but he had promised Madeline he would be here in support. Of course, that was when he was her husband.

His suit wasn't Armani, but he still cleaned up well. He'd gotten rid of the beard and hid his eyes behind a large pair of fashionable sunglasses. He was almost through the door, too, but then one photographer recognized him and began snapping pictures. Next came a barrage of questions.

"Aren't you the man who pretended to be Russell Stone?"

"What are you doing here tonight?"

"Do you feel that Christopher Stone took advantage of your illness?"

"What's your real name?"

On and on it went until he made it inside the building. But even then the photographer's lights continued to flash until he found his seat.

In the next second, the lights dimmed and the house music pumped as loud as a rock-and-roll concert and the models hit the catwalk.

Marcellus didn't know much about fashion; he just liked what he liked. However, he had to admit after an hour of watching long-legged models strut like their lives depended on it, he liked a great deal of the clothing House of Madeline created.

He recognized a few outfits from when they were just sketches on Madeline or Lysandra's desk. He swelled with pride at seeing Madeline's dream come to fruition and he hated, now more than ever, that he wasn't there for the entire process...like he said he would be.

Sensing that the event was drawing to an end, he stood, ready to slip out of the building and back into obscurity, when Lysandra, Madeline, Ariel and Russ hit the stage. Suddenly he was rooted to his seat.

Russ looked as if he'd grown two inches since he'd last seen him and Ariel was even more adorable in her dark green dress...but what had absolutely captured his attention was Madeline's extremely pregnant belly.

The audience stood with thunderous applause. Madeline and the family waved merrily to the crowd and then gave a slight bow.

Marcellus stared hard and long, willing Madeline to glance in his direction. Just as she and children pivoted to head backstage, it happened. Their gazes met and she nearly took a tumble. Lysandra helped her recover and then continued their journey.

The houselights came up and Marcellus finally blinked out of his trance. "Oh, my God."

"Are you all right?" Lysandra asked once they were safely backstage.

Madeline couldn't catch her breath. "He's here."

A crowd tried to form around Madeline to con-gratulate her, but Lysandra had to fend them off by asking for some privacy.

"He's here," Madeline kept repeating.

Lysandra led her to one of the makeup artist's empty chairs. "Who's here? You're not making any sense."

"Mommy, are you all right?" Ariel asked.

Realizing she was alarming everyone, Madeline elected to take a few deep calming breaths and paint on another smile. "Yes, baby. Mommy's fine."

Lysandra looked dubious. "Are you sure?"

"Yes. Yes." She considered the likelihood that she'd truly seen Marcellus in the audience and shook her head. "It's just probably these raging hormones."

Her cousin's worry lines deepened.

"Really." She patted Lysandra's hand and stood from the chair. "I'm okay. Time to do a little meet and greet." She turned to the children. "And then it's pizza and ice cream."

The moment she left the makeup chair, Mad-eline joined the press and the congratulating critics. Though they smiled in her face now, it was too soon to know what would actually be printed about the new fashion line.

"Congratulations, dear," Cecelia gave dramatic smooches for the camera, her current boyfriend and future husband stood beaming behind her. "Absolutely stunning. You're a hit."

"I hope so."

"Ms. Stone. Ms. Stone. How do you feel about your late husband's impersonator being here tonight?"

The question knocked the wind out of her. "What?"

"Did you know that he would be attending?"

It was her mother's turn to speak. "What?"

"You didn't know he was here?" the reporter asked.

Madeline ignored the question and turned to scan the room. The place was filling up with caterers, waiters and fashion groupies.

Then she saw him.

He stood all the way in the back, watching.

"Excuse me for a moment," she said absently to the reporter.

Cecelia grabbed her hand.

She looked over at her mother.

"Baby, are you sure?"

Tears glistened in Madeline's eyes as she nodded.

Slowly, Cecelia released her hand; fear for her daughter's fragile heart clearly in her eyes.

Madeline turned and began navigating her way through the crowd, her heart pounding. *Why was he here? What did it mean? Did he bring his family with him?*

She was just a few feet from him when she remembered her very pregnant belly. Surely the man could do math and put two and two together. She stopped, suddenly uncertain.

Marcellus moved against the flow of celebrating bodies and reached Madeline before she had a chance to retreat. Once he was standing in front of her, he had one hell of a time squeezing out one word. "Hello."

Madeline blinked, drew a deep breath and replied, "Hi."

And that was it for a few long, heart-pounding seconds. Both were overwhelmed by the other's presence that they didn't know what the next move should be. Then Madeline began with the obvious.

"You look good. I mean, well. You look well."

"You look beautiful," he said simply. "You're practically glowing."

Fresh tears stung the back of Madeline's eyes,

but this time she managed to keep them from falling. "Thank you."

Marcellus nodded and slid his hands into his pockets in an effort to look more casual than he felt. "It was a wonderful show. You should be proud." He paused. "I'm proud of you."

"Thanks... Did, uh, your family enjoy it?"

Marcellus cocked his head.

"I mean, I understand if you didn't bring them with you. I guess it would be a little awkward for me to meet your real wife."

"My wife?" he questioned. "I'm not married."

Madeline's head snapped up. "What? Of course you are. It said so in your file."

"What file?"

"Champagne?" A passing waiter inquired.

"No," Madeline and Marcellus answered in unison.

"What file?" Marcellus questioned again.

Madeline felt off-centered as she tried to understand what he was saying. "Christopher had, um, a private investigator run your fingerprints to find out who you were."

"Oh," was all he could think to say.

"The report, uh, said that you were married and had been in the military."

Marcellus nodded. "I was in the military and I was married—once."

"Once? Meaning…"

"Meaning that she passed away years ago… at the World Trade Center."

Madeline gasped. "Oh, I'm sorry. I didn't know."

"Yeah." Marcellus nodded. "Well, it was a long time ago. Another lifetime."

"Then why did you…?" The tears were storming their barrier again and then a few rebels escaped and slid down her face. "Why did you leave?"

"Because I didn't…because I don't belong in your world. I'm not a rich man. I can't buy you the finest things and—"

"I don't care about that." Madeline inched closer to him, as close as her belly would allow, and stared into his eyes. "I care about you. I fell in love with you."

Marcellus searched her eyes, looking for the truth before finally admitting, "I love you, too." He smiled and placed his hand against her belly. "Just as I'm going to love our new child."

She cried in earnest as he swept her into his arms and kissed her senseless. Hot tingles shot through her every nerve and yet she wanted to get even closer. Vaguely, she heard ripples of "oohs" and "ahs" and the steady shuttering of cameras.

However, Marcellus abruptly ended the kiss. "I think we better get you to a hospital."

"What? Why?"

"Because I think your water just broke."

"The baby is breeched," Dr. Roberts announced to his small crew in the obstetrical ward. "Let's get her prepped for emergency C-section."

An elevated Madeline Stone lay huffing and puffing on the delivery table wondering where in the hell was the epidural.

"Okay, Mrs. Stone. I need you to *stop* pushing for me."

Why did they always say that? She didn't have any control of her lower extremities. It was all she could do to ride out the waves of muscle spasms, sharp stabs of back pain and the streams of sweat burning her eyes.

Marcellus burst into the delivery room in blue scrubs. "I'm here. I'm here. How are you doing, baby?" He rushed to her side and took her hand.

Madeline's response was a high pitch scream followed by a low rabid growl. There was no doubt about it; she was having another baby that was determined to split her in half.

"It's okay, baby. You're doing a good job. I'm proud of you." With his free hand, he quickly mopped the sweat from her brow. "You look so beautiful, sweetheart. We're going to get through this together. Okay?"

Madeline nodded weakly, thrilled beyond measure to have Marcellus by her side while delivering their child.

"I must warn you," he whispered secretly. "I've never been to a Lamaze class."

"It's okay. I'm a veteran at this."

They shared a short laugh before another contraction hit. She squeezed his hand and he absorbed the pain without complaint and when the spasm subsided, he again mopped the sweat from her brow.

"There's just one thing I need to ask you before the baby arrives," he said.

"W-what's that?"

"Will you marry me? Marcellus Cougar ex-Army Major?"

"Yes," she panted. "I'd marry you no matter what your name was. I love you, Marcellus."

"And I love you." He leaned down and kissed

her moist brow. "Now, let's deliver this kid so we can get started planning our wedding."

"You got it." She crushed his hand again just as the next contraction hit.

Twenty minutes later, an eight pounds and four ounces Marcellus Joshua Cougar, Jr. made his grand entrance into the world.

Two weeks later, his parents were married at City Hall.

Epilogue

Two years later...

Christmas was the Cougars' favorite time of the year. Not only would they pile into the car and go Christmas-tree shopping, they'd also huddle together to during the Rockefeller Christmas-tree lighting, check out the New York City's ballet performance of *The Nutcracker* and, of course, overdosed on homemade, chocolate-covered s'mores.

Madeline watched her family buzz around the

Christmas tree, which had more food than actual ornaments, and smiled. It'd been confusing to the children when Marcellus returned to their lives, but in the end, they were all happy to have him back.

For a while, the children were afraid he would leave again. Russ was more distrustful than Ariel, but after a few months, he finally came around. On Marcellus and Madeline's first anniversary, Marcellus legally adopted Ariel and Russ. Officially becoming their father.

In truth, they didn't need the slip of paper. He'd always been their father where it had counted most, in his heart.

Two-year old, Marc, giggled endlessly when eleven-year Russ would saddle him on his back and crawl around the floor like a horsy or when his nine-year old sister would blow an endless stream of raspberries against his belly button.

Madeline never dreamed she could be this happy. She'd sold Stone Cold Records to a competing label and with Marcellus running the business end of House of Madeline, she and Lysandra were free to focus on the creative end of the industry. In all, they were still a glowing success.

Now, pregnant with her fourth child, Madeline

looked forward to filling her home and future with love. The first time, she'd married for money. This time, she got it right and married for love.

"Uh-oh. You're under the mistletoe," Ariel chanted. "You know what that means, Daddy. You gotta kiss Mommy."

Marcellus smiled and looked over at his wife. "Rules are rules."

"Uh-huh." Madeline slid her arms up and around his shoulders. Her eyes sparkled. "Now, shut up and kiss me."

Grinning, Marcellus leaned forward and delivered a kiss that sent her soul soaring into the heavens.

The children applauded, little Marc, too.

After surviving so much tragedy in his life, Marcellus thanked God everyday for his new and growing family. It could have only been a miracle that had brought him such a gift and he would spend the rest of his life treasuring every moment of it.

USA TODAY Bestselling Author

BRENDA
JACKSON

invites you to discover the always sexy and
always satisfying Madaris Men.

Experience where it all started…

Tonight and Forever
December 2007

Whispered Promises
January 2008

Eternally Yours
February 2008

One Special Moment
March 2008

ARABESQUE®

www.kimanipress.com

KPBJREISSUES08

USA TODAY bestselling author

BRENDA JACKSON

TONIGHT AND FOREVER

A Madaris Family novel.

Just what the doctor ordered…

After a bitter divorce, Lorren Jacobs has vowed to never give her heart again. But then she meets Justin Madaris, a handsome doctor who carries his own heartache. The spark between them is undeniable, but sharing a life means letting go of the past. Can they fight through the painful memories of yesterday to fulfill the passionate promise of tomorrow?

"Brenda Jackson has written another sensational novel… sensual and sexy—all the things a romance reader could want in a love story."
—*Romantic Times BOOKreviews* on *Whispered Promises*

Available the first week of December wherever books are sold.

ARABESQUE®

www.kimanipress.com

KPBJ0231207

following LOVE

Award-winning author

CELESTE O. NORFLEET

Desperate for a job, single mom Dena Graham only has
one option—work for sexy, charismatic Julian Hamilton.
Julian has had enough of relationships and is focused
strictly on business…until Dena walks into his life.
Now these two, who've sworn never to gamble with
their hearts again, find that when red-hot attraction
enters the picture, all bets are off!

"A story that warrants reading over and over again!"
—*Romantic Times BOOKreviews* on *One Sure Thing*

Available the first week of December
wherever books are sold.

ARABESQUE®

www.kimanipress.com KPCON0241207

Sometimes parents do know best!

Essence bestselling author

LINDA HUDSON-SMITH

*F*ORSAKING
ALL
OTHERS

They remembered each other as gawky teenagers and
had resisted their parents' meddlesome matchmaking.
But years later, when Jessica and Weston share a family ski
weekend, they discover a sizzling attraction between them.
Only, how long can romance last once they've left their
winter wonderland behind?

"A truly inspiring novel!"
—*Romantic Times BOOKreviews* on *Secrets and Silence*

*Coming the first week of December
wherever books are sold.*

KIMANI™
ROMANCE

www.kimanipress.com

KPLHS0451207

Bestselling author

Tamara Sneed

The follow-up to her acclaimed novel *At First Sight...*

At First
TOUCH

Daytime TV diva Quinn Sibley needs a comeback.
But first she needs to return to the man she left behind.
Wyatt Granger's still searching for Ms. Right—someone
quiet, shy and totally unlike this Hollywood siren who
haunts his dreams.

"At First Sight is a multilayered story that successfully
deals with sibling rivalry, family dynamics and
small-town psychology."
—*Romantic Times BOOKreviews* (4 stars)

*Coming the first week of December
wherever books are sold.*

KIMANI™
ROMANCE

www.kimanipress.com

KPTS0461207

"Devon pens a good story."
—*Romantic Times BOOKreviews* on *Love Once Again*

Favorite author

DEVON VAUGHN ARCHER

CHRISTMAS HEAT

The emotional painting of his late father seared
Aaron Pearson's soul and compelled him to meet the
artist, Deana Lamour. But her beauty and grace reawakened
in him a lust for life and enabled him to finally confront
the ghosts of his past.

*Coming the first week of December
wherever books are sold.*

KIMANI™
ROMANCE

www.kimanipress.com

KPDVA0471207

A volume of heartwarming devotionals
that will nourish your soul...

NORMA DeSHIELDS BROWN

Joy

COMES THIS MORNING

Norma DeShields Brown's life suddenly changed
when her only son was tragically taken from her
by a senseless act. Consumed by grief, she began
an intimate journey that became
Joy Comes This Morning.

Filled with thoughtful devotions, Scripture readings
and words of encouragement, this powerful book
will guide you on a spiritual journey that will sustain
you throughout the years.

*Available the first week of November
wherever books are sold.*

www.kimanipress.com   KPNDB0351107

GET THE GENUINE LOVE
YOU DESERVE...

NATIONAL BESTSELLING AUTHOR
Vikki Johnson

Addicted to COUNTERFEIT LOVE

Many people in today's world are unable to recognize
what a genuine loving partnership should be and
often sabotage one when it does come along. In this
moving volume, Vikki Johnson offers memorable
words that will help readers identify destructive love
patterns and encourage them to demand the love
that they are entitled to.

Available the first week of October wherever books are sold.

www.kimanipress.com   KPVJ0381007